Empire of Thorns

SERIES

The Thorns Mark

The Willing Queen

PART TWO

By Vioshed

Copyright © 2021 Vioshed

All rights reserved

The characters and events portrayed in this book are fictitious. Any similarity to real persons, living or dead, is coincidental and not intended by the author.
I do not own the picture on the cover

No part of this book may be reproduced, or stored in a retrieval system, or transmitted in any form or by any means, electronic, mechanical, photocopying, recording, or otherwise, without express written permission of the publisher.

ISBN-13: 9798754297661

Cover design by: Art Painter
Library of Congress Control Number: 2018675309
Printed in the United States of America

Contents

Copyright
Introduction
Chapter 1 — 1
Chapter 2 — 10
Chapter 3 — 19
Chapter 4 — 28
Chapter 5 — 37
Chapter 6 — 46
Chapter 7 — 56
Chapter 8 — 66
Chapter 9 — 76
Chapter 10 — 86
Chapter 11 — 96
Chapter 12 — 106
Chapter 13 — 116
Chapter 14 — 125
Chapter 15 — 135
Epilogue — 145

Social media	155
Books In This Series	157
Books By This Author	159

Introduction

This is the sequel to the book, The Thorns King's wife

Moriah believes that her suffering will have no end. Life in the Underworld is slowly killing her. All her hopes and will to live are fading away. Nothing matters but to fulfil her destiny.

The fight between heaven and hell can break out at any moment. Armaloth will do whatever it takes to make the prophecy come true, and not even the god above himself will stand in his way.

This book is the end of Armaloth and Moriah's story and has sensitive themes for some readers, including scenes of blood, violence, sex and devious consent.

Chapter 1

Destroy them

Armaloth

After leaving my wife asleep in our chambers, I made my way to the throne chamber. Now that Moriah is safe and out of harm's way, it's time to deal with the clans once and for all.

My mind went over and over again to what the Dragon Demon told me, the clans were organized, all against me. Forming a council, what did the Dragon call them? Ah! Yes, "The Council of Seven" is pathetic. And with the queen in power, let's just say they might have the upper hand over me, in case I didn't know, but Oh! Surprise, I know. Those damn traitors won't know what hit them when I'm done with them. And as for my queen, let's just say, her reign will be very short. For now, I will gather the demons I need to put an end to this. As I raised my arms, I invoked the ancient powers of the underworld. "Thanatos, my loyal servant, my faithful demon, come to me, the God of the underworld calls you." A ball of black smoke formed in front of me, this energy is incredible.

It has been a long time since I have experienced such a beautiful force as this, death. From the black cloud emerged the creature that I was waiting for. Dressed in a black cloak, carrying the sword of death fastened to his belt. With his black wings spread towards me. Thanatos knelt before me. "My king, your servant is here to assist you." I approached him and put my hand on his shoulder, signalling him to get up, and he did. The god of death, the Knight of darkness, the demon who carries out my mandate with his sword, my executioner.

"Thanatos, I need you to take care of a problem." I brought him up to speed on everything the Dragon Demon told me, and what had happened to Persephone's crown. He will be the one to lead those traitors of the council of seven to their doom, "I will destroy them, for you, my lord."

"Now, before you take care of the seven clan leaders, I need you to bring before me one demon from each clan. I don't care who you choose, but they must be true to me and fear me. No one should know about this, and once you have brought them before me, I will take care of the rest." My infernal executioner bowed his head in reverence and disappeared without saying more. I returned to my throne and my thorny branches zigzagged along my body. Then, I felt her energy flowing through me, but not only that, I could also feel my wife's presence through the bond. Then, closing my eyes, I was filled with her presence.

My wife was uneasy and upset, which made me smile, she sure is bored. But I know how to entertain her and keep her busy for a while. Until I solve this problem with the clans, she will have to remain locked in my catacombs. I cannot risk her. She is very important and valuable, and nothing can take her away from me. I will make the prophecy come true.

My daughters and sons will conquer the worlds and no demon, god, or angel will be able to prevent it. I still have something else to do, before returning to my wife, "Anton." My servant, in a matter of seconds, materialized before me, "My lord, almighty and powerful, I am at your service." I have to know what has been going on while I have been away, "Give me your report, and I want it with details."

"My master and lord, of course. The queen has been very busy meeting with her advisers. She installed her throne in the chamber of lost souls." Very convenient for her, and my servant continued. "The leaders of the Bloodrink and Poissonarm clan requested an audience too. Unfortunately, the power of my queen is too powerful for your humble servant to penetrate her barrier." Damn, that demon thinks she is very clever. My eyes began to glow from the energy I was generating. I couldn't contain my fury, and I sent a shock wave towards the wall in front of me. My servant did not dare to move from his place, if I wanted, he would be disintegrated "ARRR! Continue "

" Y-yes my l-oor-d and m-ast-er, the meeting lasted one hour and fifty minutes. Half an hour before ending, two demons joined them. One of them is my queen's trusted adviser, his name is Headeath. The other demon I had not seen before, that is all I have to report, Lord and Master." So they're already moving, okay, okay, Drickblood, okay.

"Anton, keep watching her. Whatever demons are seen with the queen, let me know right away. Give me a list of all the advisers she has in her service. And those close to the leader of the Bloodrink and Poissonarm clans. "

I will finish them all, I will have no mercy, no one who dares to challenge me will live to tell the tale. "My master, there is something else that I have to inform you." I waved my hand as a sign that he has permission to speak. "We have discovered the reason for the death of Poissona. The representative of the Poissonarm Clan in the tribulation games. The expert discovered that her body was drained." I narrow my eyes and raise my head at this news.

I am beginning to connect the dots. "The demon of ceremonies suspects that my queen had something to do. Since piercings at the base of the neck were found, and they are consistent with the bite of a vampire demon." I suspected the same, but I let my servant continue. "The theory that he is handling is that the queen absorbed Poissona's poisonous powers. With the aim of piercing the invincible skin of the Cerberus. The poison itself would not harm him, but if it would momentarily weaken his skin. This would be the perfect opportunity for my queen to pierce him with her fangs and draw even a drop of blood. And with that, absorb the powers of the great beast. "

That's right, it was a brilliant plan. "Servant, I'm going to bring the hellhound back. He will surely have a pending account to settle in the future. If the queen has any complaints, she will have to do with me, understood?" Anton nodded his head. I waved my hand for him to back off. He touched the ground with his forehead and vanished.

I was about to retreat to my catacombs when a presence materialized before me. My Queen appeared in the middle of a dense black cloud, as well, I could feel energy and magic that I did not recognize. What I could say for sure is that this vampire was gaining a lot of power. Her mere presence could match the strongest demons in the underworld.

Sadly, Persephone's crown protects her from me. It is the symbol that identifies her as the beloved of the king of the underworld. However, I had seen through the ghoulish plans of my enemies. It was brilliant, just brilliant. At the moment, I cannot attack her. I need a compelling pretext to get the crown to abandon her. Everything will happen in time; I can only be patient.

As Drickblood strode towards me, her steps were powerful and determined. This demon has grown so much in power that it would be fair to say that if she faces me in a battle, she would cause me some trouble. Therefore, I need to end her as soon as possible. Lean my head against the back of my throne, and silently wait for her to speak. "My dear king, I salute you. I have waited days for this moment. You have been so busy lately, and I have missed you so much that my black heart is in pain. Her eyes have become a vortex of destruction, feeding on death and hunger.

I know that very well, mine feed on the same thing, "My queen, to what do I owe your presence?" Drickblood nodded her head and moved close to me. She leaned closer and touched my hand with hers. I immediately moved. She raised her hands in surrender and said, "My beloved king of the underworld. As you know, the clans are nervous. I have been in direct contact with them, listening to their concerns." HMM! So she already knows I'm spying on her. Interesting

"We need to conceive our heir. And you know it well, my lord and master Armaloth. I do not understand what is keeping you away from that glorious moment. Our powers will be immeasurable and everything will be focused on our creation. A demon that will have no equal."

In that instant, I felt slight dizziness, my eyes began to blur. I blinked several times to adjust my vision, but it was useless. My thorny branches began to snake around me, putting a protective barrier around me. Something is not right. I tried to get up, but my legs did not support me, I fell on my knees. But managed to support me with my hands so as not to fall on my face. I raised my head and I saw Drickblood standing in front of me, looking at me with disdain. Between teeth, I spoke: "What did you do to me?"

"My king, what are you talking about? It seems that you don't feel well. Let me help you." She approached me, and I moved my hand so that she would not touch me. She pouted and in a mocking tone said to me, "Hey, hey, my king, that's not nice. You have to let me help you. At the end of the day, we are united. I am your true wife. The queen, the ruler of the underworld." The spinning of my head increased, my vision became blurrier. And I remarked with horror how the thorny branches lowered their guard and remained still beside me. "The thorny branches are aware of how much I love you, they know that I am yours. Together, we will be a happy family."

CHAPTER 1

"My, my! We will take care of all your concerns soon, so don't worry." Those words brought me back to Moriah. I must find her before it is too late. I invoked my power, but nothing happened. Something happened with my power when she touched me. "Do not resist, do not fight. Allow everything to happen as it should." I was losing focus quickly when I felt something break inside me. At that moment, I turned to see Drickblood. But she looked different, and I saw her for who she was, the real Persephone, my queen. Once the strength returned to my body, I stood up and walked towards her.

Then, without thinking any longer, I took her neck. Snatched her mouth, and our tongues intertwined in a lusty, deadly dance. The kiss abruptly ended, and I grabbed her shoulders and turned her so that her back was to me. With my knee, I spread her legs and penetrated her without delay. My thrusts were brutal, and Drickblood received each one with equal force. Our energy swirled around us, immense and powerful. Suddenly, my queen shifted position, now riding me. As she impaled herself time after time, I was contemplating her from here. Then, the image of Moriah briefly entered my mind. I allowed it to pass and continued enjoying the encounter. We did it in all positions and everywhere, our meeting was wild and hard, so we are demons.

We ended the two on the floor panting, both catching our breath. Drickblood sat down and was the one who broke the silence. "My King, I will never tire of having you inside. I have looked forward to this day for years, and it has finally arrived. It was very bad of you to keep me away from you and all the things that are important, all because of that human. " Ah, the human! Yes, Moriah, "Do not worry my queen, the human will serve her purpose and nothing else, it is you that I want by my side." It was true, we would be invincible, and our heir would be the most powerful of them all. My enemies will fall like dead flies before me. We will be known as the most lethal rulers of all time. We will live in everyone's mind, our names will inspire only fear.

"My king, I would like to bring my throne here, to the throne chamber, next to yours." My queen passed her sharp nail across my chest, her eyes displaying intense desire. "Whatever you want, my queen, whatever you want." She smiled wickedly, but I didn't think anything about it. "I also want to live with you, so that we share the same roof. What do you say, love? Will you invite me to your catacombs?" I watched her carefully as I leaned on my elbows, my desire to have her surpassing my reason. As I approached her mouth, I bit her passionately, drawing blood, Mm!! Moriah's tasty blood, Moriah Mm! The human occupied my thoughts and I did not understand why.

I decided at that moment to forget everything and take my queen again. We did not leave the throne chamber for a long time. When we finished, I stood up and offered her my hand. She took it confidently and got up from the floor. I held her hand tight as we transferred to the catacombs. I saw the human in the distance once the cloud of smoke had dispersed. She was curled up, her eyes were red, and her skin looked pale.

I do not remember seeing her like this before I left. However, all I thought about right now was having my queen, and nothing else. Moriah looked up and saw us with visible shock on her face. I looked at her foot and noticed that the thorny branch was still holding it. Well, I will keep it like that, restricted until I have use of her. As we approached her, the tree of knowledge immediately went on guard. Creating a barrier between humans and us.

This filled me with rage. With my power I forced the branches to lower their guard, they remained inert by her side. This shouldn't be happening. So with resentment in my voice, I spoke, "What did you do with my tree, human? Why is it attacking me? MY OWN TREE, ARRRR!" As I ran over to her with lightning speed, I grabbed her by the neck and lifted her into the air. Her feet dangling from her helplessness, and her weak, small hands struggling to free her neck. Her eyes filled with tears begged me to release her, and her face was beginning to look purple and pathetic. I threw her away from my presence, her fall was stopped by one of the branches. Which placed her carefully on the ground. With disdain, I saw how the surrounding branches snaked around her, curling all over her, comforting.

When I was about to go against her again, my queen stopped me, "My love, don't worry about her. It wouldn't be worth the trouble. She is here only to give you the army. Be careful with your strength, or you can permanently damage her." My queen is right, she has to give me what I need, "You are right, my queen." I approached the human and kicked her in the back hard several times. Thanks to me, her body is more resistant and can heal faster than a normal human, so I don't have to deny myself the fun.

Chapter 2

I'm going to die here
Moriah

I've been here for days, or so I think. I don't really know how long it's been since Armaloth confined me to his catacombs. Not only that but I'm chained to a wall, like a wild animal. My neck is shackled with a metal chain that is hooked to the wall. It is so short that I can hardly lie on the floor to sleep without hanging myself.

My feet and hands are chained too, and my body is not good. I have a lot of pain in my stomach. From the first day that I felt a pain piercing my insides until today, it has not stopped. All the time it is present, the only moment it stops is when the king is resting. And I am having a hard time recovering from the damage they are inflicting on me. I feel very sick, my body starts to feel hungry and there is nothing I can do, no one has fed me in all this time. The times when someone approaches, it is to hurt me and make fun of me.

The few times I am released from these chains is to hurt me. Why did everything turn out the way it did? What caused Armaloth to change his attitude towards me? I was immersing myself in my misery and thoughts when suddenly the king and queen appeared. The two of them started having sex in front of me. It was very violent, but it seems they are both enjoying it.

Looking at the other side, as I always do when this happens. I notice this pain as well. Which seems to dig into my very being whenever they are doing it. It doesn't leave me until they have finished. I don't know what this means, but I doubt that I will last longer in these conditions. The Queen was lying in the arms of her king when she turned to see me, and her evil look told me that it would be very bad for me soon. Then she pointed her claw at me and said something to the king. He nodded and then got up. As fear gathered at the tip of my stomach, my body began to tremble. And terror seized me so rapidly that I couldn't think straight.

He grabbed my neck and released the chains, and dragged me over to where the queen was and threw me to the floor at her feet. Her eyes were afire with hunger. And she licked her lips before grabbing my hair, pulling my head back and biting my neck harshly.

My strength was nothing compared to them, it was useless to fight. I remained motionless, letting her feed on me. The pain that her fangs caused me could not be described. My screams did not bother her, on the contrary. That, excited her more. As the vampire sucked my blood, the king took her from behind. The pain in my stomach started right away. My tears wouldn't stop coming out, I felt like it was my end. But it never came, they always made sure to stop before crossing that line. They kept me alive for their purposes. If I could take my life, I would do it without thinking. The king roared, shaking the place. I knew he had reached his pick. The queen abruptly released me and threw her head back. I ended up a few steps from them. My body could not move, I was without strength and breath. I was like a dirty rag thrown on the floor. My cheeks smeared with dirt along with my tears.

The king was watching me from a distance, he moved a hand and my body went flying straight towards him. He grabbed my hair and turned my face down, opened my legs with his knee and penetrated me. I gasped, my breath shortened, I couldn't get the air into my lungs. He rammed me over and over with his hard member. The pain I felt from my body being torn was a lot. My mind began to rave, I began to see black dots. My tears clouded my vision, and I only could close my eyes. I wasn't able to hold them open until I lost myself in nothingness.

****

Little by little I opened my eyes since the pain in my body did not let me escape from this reality any longer. My mouth was dry, my tongue was sticking to my palate, my lips were split and crusted, I urgently needed water. I turned my head to see around me, luckily I was alone.

My neck was bad, it hurt more than other times, this was not the first time that she fed on me. But now the pain is multiplying, and I am not healing as before. The wounds are fresh, and the pain just does not leave me. My body is giving up, I know that. Those wounds that have not yet healed are infected, I see pus, and they smell bad. No one can help, nor do I believe they will or can. What the king says must be obeyed. And his queen has a great influence on him. Before all this, I thought my situation wasn't bad, when the king called me his wife and me, my husband.

Now I would like everything to go back to how it was before. The only thing left for me is to wait for them to make a mistake and end my life. I tried to sit up, but it was impossible, so, what I did was turn on my side and see if there was water anywhere. When I moved, I felt a terrible tug on my neck. With a lot of effort, I touched the wound with my hand, and it trembled from the effort. I felt wet, I turned to see what it was, and it came out full of blood. It was not little, it also felt like it was running from my neck to my chest. This was good, maybe I'll bleed out and die.

I also noticed something else, I was bleeding from between my legs, that's why my abdomen feels so swollen. The king must have damaged it badly. Usually, after he takes me, I only bleed for a while, but now, that is not the case. My suspicions were true, my body is dying, but what I need right now is water. I could not see anywhere, so I turned my back and closed my eyes. There was no point in being awake. I was about to sleep again when I heard noises in the distance. My heart was beating with intensity, the fear was great, they did a good job tattooing it in my mind. The king and queen materialized as always, and they were doing something or other. After a while, I felt the king approach me. Despite everything, I could still feel the connection we once shared. It was almost imperceptible, but it was still there.

I didn't open my eyes, even if I wanted to, because it was a lot of work. So I stayed put without moving, doing nothing, until he spoke, "Human, get up." Since I could not answer him, he kicked me several times. He kicked me so hard that I ended up several meters away. And then I heard his footsteps approaching, then he grabbed my hair and lifted me into the air. The pain in my body resumed, and only a small moan left my lips. I opened my eyes as best I could. Although my vision was blurry, I could still identify his silhouette.

His face was right in front of mine, "Why are you not healing humans? What is wrong with you that my power is not reaching you?" I sincerely hoped he wasn't expecting an answer from me, because I doubt I could articulate one. But it was the queen who intervened, "The human probably needs to eat something or what humans do. It hadn't occurred to me before."

However, the king shook his head in denial and said, "No, my queen. Since she came to my kingdom, she never needed any sustenance. It was my power that kept her, now I see that something isn't right."

"Well, let's try it and see if it works, if not, we'll find another solution." The queen grabbed me by the throat and pulled me out of the king's hands. She threw me aside, and my head hit the ground hard. She started kissing him and the situation got worse. They ended up having sex as usual in front of me. However, this time the king did not force himself upon me. I must look awful, so he decided to let me go. Now my head was buzzing, the blow must have been strong enough to cause me real damage. I lost consciousness and did not know anything else.

****

Upon waking, I discovered water and food on the ground, so I twisted my neck so that my tongue would reach it. I lick it from the ground as if I were an animal. But at this point, nothing mattered to me anymore. And with the food, I didn't bother. I was so exhausted and weak that despite being so hungry, I couldn't move to grab it. I spent a few days, in which neither the queen nor the king bothered me. Sometimes, I found water and food scattered around me, and other times when they found me awake, they threw it at me.

Until one day, the king approached me and dragged me to the pond by the hair. He threw me in, and ordered me to clean up. I did the best I could. And when I finished, he ordered me to get out of the water. Then, he directed me to the wall where he has always kept me restrained. This time it was a little different because he tied my hands and held them with a chain that hung from the ceiling. He lifted me up and left me there, hanging.

After he left me there for a while, my shoulders gave out. My body was in pain, and I was too weak to do anything. But sudden noises make me aware again. As I turned my head to see what was happening. Several disgusting creatures appeared from the cloud of smoke.

I started crying. The helplessness and the knowledge that they would do horrible things to me was eating me inside. And one of them starts to speak. "My king, we appreciate very much that you have given us the honour of seeing the human. We know how much she means to you. We only want to be sure that everything is fine." Then, only silence, but then I hear steps approaching me, "Poissonaro, you don't have to worry. I only have eyes for my queen. T human doesn't mean anything to me. At any moment, she will become pregnant and start breeding my warriors. That is the only thing that keeps her alive."

The queen spoke next, "That is right, Clan leader. My king only has eyes for me. And as a demonstration, our master will let you all play with her. As long as you do not damage her irreparably. It has cost us a bit of work to bring her back to health." Another monster spoke, "Is it true, my king and my lord? Can we have a bit of fun with the human? We can't always get a chance to play with the mother of the invincible army." His tone sounded a bit teasing to me, but at that moment I already knew what to expect. My tears ran down my cheeks freely. Nothing could save me from what awaited me.

"Doomerth, I warn you that no seeds can touch her. That's only for me." No one spoke after that until someone cleared his throat and said, "Of course not, my lord and master. No one would dare to touch something of yours without your permission. I assure you, my king, that no one will touch her that way." The queen chimed in. "Well, we've reached an agreement, no touching. That is why I suggest this." I heard a weird noise, but I didn't know what it was. By then, my body was covered in sweat. The waiting was destroying me. Not knowing what they wanted to do to me was devastating to my mind. I didn't have to wait long. Because my back was beaten with something that could have been a whip or a chain. I choked on the scream that it could not get out. The next blow fell in the middle of the back. This time I screamed with such force that everyone who was there began to mock and laugh at my suffering.

CHAPTER 2

The blows continued to rain on me. Some struck several times in the same place. It seemed that they took turns between them. My crying did not reach their deaf ears. No one had mercy on me My strength was leaving me again. I could no longer distinguish what was happening anymore. I only felt the pain in my back. Blood began to come out of the wounds. Not only that, but I could see how it dripped through my legs, and they ended up being absorbed by the dirt.

I also felt blows on my head, a lash reached my cheek, breaking my skin. There was no place that was not marked now. My voice ended. I had nothing else to scream, my tears also ended. I had to close my eyes to wait for everything to reach the final moments of my life.

In the distance, I heard a shout saying, "Enough." I didn't make out anything else. After that, there was only silence. Until I felt someone unleash me and let me fall to the ground. Nobody assisted me, nobody did anything for me. My life was about to end. And that is why I was happy. I cried in silence. I felt the few tears pass my eyelids, finally. Not only that, but I heard some voices say something and some noises, but I could no longer understand anything.

Then everything was quiet, everyone had left the place, leaving me to my fate. I was waiting for my end, but from nowhere, I felt a presence that seemed familiar to me. I could feel his suffering, he was sad for me. Furthermore, I did not remember how or where, but we already knew each other.

Tring to lift my head, I wanted to see with all my heart the person in front of me. I tried to open my eyes, but everything was blurry. But in that moment I thought my mind was playing tricks on me. What I could see was a large black silhouette, with fire in its eyes and legs. It was not a person, but a horse. I tried to reach out my hand to touch him, but I couldn't. The horse must have sensed my intentions because he approached me very carefully. His footsteps calmed me down, I knew I would be fine with him. For some reason, his presence comforted me. He reached out to me, and with his snout, he gently shook my head, letting me know that he was there.

I smiled a little, and at least someone would be with me in my last moments. And before succumbing to death I managed to say to him in a broken voice "Th-a-nk-s."

Chapter 3

The Realization
Armaloth

"My master, we need your authorization to send a contingent of demons to the outside world. We want to bring more human slaves. The ones that have arrived are not enough. Our clan prefers to feed on human blood, and we can easily overpower them." Blooderek, the clan leader, has been here long enough to enrage me just hearing his voice. His demands have increased in recent weeks. If it weren't for my queen suggesting this reunion, I'd be somewhere else enjoying her.

They want more humans, the last lot was quite large. Around a thousand living humans were brought from their world to serve them. The members of this clan enjoy human blood more than demonic blood. But I am beginning to get tired of them. This would never have happened before. But since my queen asked me, I have no choice but to please her. She also asked me to revoke the order to bring the Cerberus back. She thinks it is not necessary. Since our reign is powerful enough to contain any entry or exit from my kingdom.

So I had to give in to that too, and this is the result. This court is turning into a circus. Any demon feels entitled to come here and demand whatever comes to mind, like this one in front of me. I need to put an order as soon as possible. The only thing that is stopping me at the moment is my queen. "No more humans, Clan Leader, you will have to make it with what you have. And I assure you that I will not authorize any more for a while. You may go now." The leading clan did not receive my ultimatum very well.

His face contorted in fury, but he knew he must stay in control. "My lord and king. My queen specifically asked me for a new lot of humans. She intends to use them at her convenience. I would not want to fail her. Reconsider your answer, my master. They are only humans, all of them will be used for our benefit."

"INSOLENT," I formed a ball of energy and directed it towards him. The demon was hit in the face and was thrown several meters away. I got up from my throne and went towards him. I watched him with disgust and disdain. The upper part of his body was disfigured. It will be difficult for him to recover from this.

"GET OUT," I yelled in his face, making my chamber rumble with the impact of my voice. The demon nodded in acceptance and vanished. I returned to my throne and leaned my head on the back. My thorny branches don't behave as before. They no longer curled around my body, and they no longer snaked when they saw me.

I know something is wrong since the day my queen touched my hand. But as much as I want to think about something, nothing comes to mind. The only thing I can think of, is to stick myself into her. My queen. My number one priority is her. Although sometimes something in the deepest part of my head tells me that she is not the one I should worry about.

All this is confusing me. Sometimes out of nowhere I see the image of Moriah in my mind. But it disappears just as it came. Like a fleeting flash. Another thing is the headaches that I constantly get when I spend a lot of time with my queen. It is a double-edged sword. On the one hand, I need her and on the other, I cannot be with her for long. It is imperative that I find out what is wrong with me. I cannot discuss this with anyone, especially my queen. Knowing who I can trust will be difficult since I cannot afford to reveal my weakness.

It is as if I can smell them in the air, the smell of betrayal intensifies as I know they are nearby, lurking. It makes me feel weak. Just to think that I shouldn't have agreed to the clan leaders' request for proof that the human was not a threat to our kingdom. The queen, however, intervened by convincing me that keeping the demons together was necessary.

Moreover, I reluctantly agreed. Because I knew I must appease them somehow. My queen assured me that it was the right thing to do, as we wanted them on our side. So I transported myself to my catacombs. Seeing her, I felt something briefly, but it immediately disappeared. I forced her to clean herself in the pond, as I could see that her wounds were spoiling. The water in the pond has special properties. That is why I did it. Then, chain her to the ceiling and went to collect the clan leaders. Upon returning and seeing her hanging defenceless, I saw their lust running deep through the minds of these demons. I could also smell the anticipation of the pain they would inflict on her. This made me feel bad, but I didn't know why. She was just an instrument.

The first time the whip fell, I could feel her pain. Even though it was only a flash of despair. As soon as I realized her body couldn't resist any longer, I halted everything we were doing.

I had to get those demons out of my catacombs as soon as possible, so I left her lying there on the ground. Now that I am thinking of her, I will go and see that she's fine, or at least breathing. I cannot let this ruin my plans. My Agalariept materialized just as I was about to transport myself. I had time to not see him. Like my thorny branches, he kept his distance from me. As he trotted toward me, his eyes flashed with fury, and I was unable to determine his intentions. Therefore, I waited to see what he would do. He whined and blew smoke from his nose.

I saw that he was upset, and it was with me. Nevertheless, he surprised me by approaching me and resting his nose on my shoulder, as he always did. My throne suddenly snaked around me, as well as my Agalariept, and I was surprised by that as well. We created powerful energy that had never been felt before. The power that was accumulating within me was incomparable. So strong and powerful, that I felt something break.

A red vapour poured from my nose, spreading into the air. And I was paralysed when I saw the reality for the first time. My forehead was drenched in a cold sweat,.but

CHAPTER 3

What had I done? No, no, no, Moriah. I got up suddenly and transported myself to my catacombs. "Moriah," I yelled her name and headed towards the place where I left her. She was not there. How could this have happened? I wandered over and over again while holding my head in my hands. "MORIAH!" I screamed desperately. At this point, I stopped. I needed to calm down and think. As I searched every corner of the room, I found nothing. So I decided to go back in time to find out what had happened.

I invoked Cronus powers, which came to me like lightning. It crossed my entire body, starting from my head and ending on my feet. As I recalled the moment when we were whipping her. Everything happened like in a film. I was like a spectator watching it all unfold. I observed everything carefully. The satisfied face that Drickblood had every time the whip struck Moriah made my stomach turn. The clan leaders sadistically gloated over my wife's suffering.

And I allowed it, I also looked at my face, my expression was blank. Deep inside, I knew that this was a mistake. But I let myself be manipulated by that poisonous snake. I, the mighty king of the underworld, the god of demons, was vilely deceived. Even though my anger was reaching a point of no return, I decided to go further back in time.

I watched helplessly as we tortured Moriah all this time. From that time when Drickblood was bored and decided it was a good idea to hit the target with Moriah. She and I stabbed her several times in various parts of her body, knowing that she could heal in a short time.

Also, observe when we kicked her for something that she

did not do quickly enough for our liking. That beating was brutal. I remember that she took many days to get up. By that time, her body was no longer healing as before. The wounds remained for a long time just like the pain. I saw it all, and my blood boiled with resentment towards Drickblood.

I only had one thought, and that was revenge. Still, I went to the part where it all began. She approached me and when she touched my hand, my body reacts to something she did. I have to know how was it possible for a lower demon like her to control me. Going further back in time. I remembered that my servant told me The Queen had met her trusted advisor, as well as an unknown demon. So I went to that moment.

In the chamber of lost souls. Sitting on her throne. She was speaking to the Blooderek clan leader when a stranger and her assistant appeared in her presence. The advising demon bowed, but the other one did not. The queen got up and went to them, so I was shocked when she was the one bowing to the stranger. He was covered with a cloak that concealed his identity with a spell, so that is why my servant had no idea who he was. They spoke for about half an hour, just as my servant had informed me. And I was able to see through his mask when he turned to the Clan Leader with his face exposed to me. His power could no longer fool me, I saw through his mask.

It's him! I recognize him! Now I understand everything, and I know how that vampire managed to put a curse on me by just touching me. It all makes sense. The dragon demon's help, the seven clans against me, the queen's coronation. The stranger conspiring with them all.

The heavens will pay dearly for this intervention. Nathanael, the disciple of the archangel Michael, was the stranger who met with the queen. Because the heavens are conspiring to overthrow me and leave the queen or my heir in my place. That is why the urgency to procreate one with the queen, but I know now. They want to prevent me from forming my invincible army and take away my right to conquer everything. It will never happen, never. Before I do anything else, I must find Moriah. That is what is most important at this time.

I need to look deeper into this. I watched the scene where I left her lying on the ground for a while and saw that she was addressing someone. Her head turned toward the direction, and she extended her hand, but nothing happened. And a moment later, she smiled and muttered something. Then she closed her eyes and disappeared.

There is nothing else, someone is blocking me again. I was transported back to my reality because I had already seen everything I needed. My biggest fear was that Moriah had been taken by some celestial being. I returned to the throne chamber and my thorny branches welcomed me. My infernal steed stood on two legs and whinnied. Our energy was in tune again. I'm so glad I woke up from that curse, now I have to put together a plan to destroy them all. The best thing I can do is continue with the charade. Now that I know everything, it will be easier to destroy their plans.

And I won't risk being cursed again, the best solution is to feign ignorance and show them that I am on their side. Those damned members of the council of seven. They wanted to manipulate me so that I would do whatever they wanted. I am ashamed to know that they did it for a while. I approached my steed and said in a low voice, "I have to find my wife. Not only that, but I need you to help me, I don't trust anyone, I don't know who is with me right now."

My Agalariept looked at me suspiciously. I never thought the time would come when my own demon steed would stop trusting me. But I deserve it, for falling blindly into the enemy's trap. I know why he is like this. Yes, I hurt his mistress without mercy, and I let others hurt her too. So I said, "I'm fine now, nothing can stop me from taking revenge on our enemies, and I swear I will take care of her with my life."

My demon horse threw its head back and whinnied. I convinced him. I shook my head in disbelief and said, "Show me." He froze completely, and his eyes rolled back, he began to project what had happened after I left her. I saw my steed materialize in the catacombs and approach Moriah. Now I know who she smiled at and who she was trying to reach. My Agalariept approached her, and with his snout shook her head. Moriah thanked him and immediately lost consciousness.

This was hard to watch, but I am Armaloth, and I will emerge ahead of all circumstances. The next thing that happened, my steed enveloped Moriah's inert body with his energy. He transported her to the dimension of the dragon beast, of all places. He must have chosen the Dragon demon because here all are enemies. I turned to see my horse with a questioning face. He moved his head up and down and turned around, not paying me any more attention.

Apparently, my horse trusts the Dragon Demon blindly. He would not send his mistress to a place where she was in danger, so I will have to go with the flow. Well done my horse, well done, I thought. I know that Moriah will be fine with the Dragon, and I trusted him to help her to recover from everything we did to her. When I finish with those traitors I will go to take her back, my wife will return to her master and lord, where she belongs.

Chapter 4

The queen will fall
Armaloth

I stayed in the throne chamber for a little longer, thinking about what to do. I was enjoying the company of my thorny branches and my infernal steed. Not only that, but I preyed on that time, to be with them, I wanted to make up for the lost time.

Or just that, we also can get stronger at the same time. Suddenly, my Agalariept was upset, through the bond. I could feel his hostility, an enemy was about to arrive. In a matter of seconds, my queen materialized before me. My faithful steed stood on guard along with my thorny branches. I immediately calmed them. Since I do not want anyone to suspect anything. They understood and let me do my job. Drickblood approached me seductively. Sat on my legs and kissed me with passion and hunger.

I had the immense desire to throw her to the ground and cut her into pieces, but I have to hold it back, my reign is at stake. She ended the kiss and got up, walked over to my steed and touched his nose. I felt all the resentment he felt towards her, but fortunately, he remained contained.

Then she turned around looking at me and said, "Hear what happened with the Blooderek clan leader. I know they have been asking a lot of you lately, my king, but it is necessary."

She paused for a moment and continued, "Humans are good slaves, also good food. My beloved king, lord of the underworld, reconsider your position." She walked towards me and began to touch my member. I closed my eyes, containing my anger, she took it as a sign that I was enjoying her touch. Then she bows her head taking my member between her lips and licked the tip. My fingers urge me to strangle her. I wanted to crush her skull and turn it into dust, right here, I was so close to pulverizing her.

My tunnel vision was fixed on the back of her neck. I was about to go for it when my thorny branch tangled around my ankle, squeezing hard. That brought me to reality immediately. I threw my head back and closed my eyes. Took several deep breaths to release the tension that was very close to exploding. I closed my mind to any thought, but Moriah's perfect body suddenly appeared. I remembered her face, full of satisfaction and pleasure when I flooded her body with my seeds.

Her walls were squeezing me, sucking every last drop of my vitality. Her mouth opens in ecstasy, and her blood dripping from my fangs, her unmatched taste, Uh! Yea! Moriah, Uff! AAAH! My pleasure hit me hard. I squeezed my eyes so intensely. I exploded with such force that I felt jet after jet come out without stopping. Ah! I leaned my head back and gave myself a few seconds to recover, and when I opened them I saw what was in front of me. My blood turned to ice, Drickblood's face greeted me with a smile full of satisfaction. It was so disgusting to see her, that I stood up so abruptly, that she fell back from the impulse. She shot me a questioning look about my action, but she didn't say anything. She just got up and approached me, touched my chest with her hand and brought her nose to my neck. I immediately grabbed her hair, forcing her head back, she gave a little cry of surprise. But I took the moment to divert her attention from me.

I kissed her as I had before. As if I did not know of her betrayal, as if she had not allied herself with the angels to overthrow me. That was all I had to do to keep from throwing up in her face. She, in response, put her arms around my neck and reciprocated the kiss. I finished the kiss and returned to my throne. I sat down and answered what she came to tell me. "My queen, I had missed you. I already needed this," Referring to the sexual encounter a moment ago. "And to answer your question, no, I will not let any more living humans come to my kingdom. This has nothing to do with clan leaders."

"It's very simple, this place is the underworld. The livings do not live here, only the souls in penance and demons, but living humans, no." The queen was thinking hard about how to answer this, but I noticed that she was speechless. That's right, you have nothing Drickblood, nothing.

Apparently, she gave up for the moment, because the next thing she asked me made me very uncomfortable. "A while ago I went to the catacombs, I did not see the human anywhere, what did you do with her?" I have to feign indifference, and make this credible, "The human was in very bad condition. I had to send her to someone who knew how to treat her kind." And to make the matter more convincing, I added, "You know how important it is to our plans. If she died or was permanently disabled, she could not fulfil the prophecy. From now on, we have to be more careful with her." She nodded her head in acceptance, apparently believed everything, and now it was my turn to press. "My queen, now tell me, what have you been doing all this time? I have waited for you for hours, you know how I need you, right? "

She widened her eyes in surprise, and quickly masked it with a smile. "Oh! Does my King miss me? Pouting when finished. Unpleasant creature, I have to suck it up. Because I need to know what they have planned, and I know very well how to achieve it. No one can resist my powers, and less a demon like her. I will make her my puppet, I will use this same traitor as a spy, and after I get what I want, the queen will fall. I got up from my throne and walked slowly towards her. Not only that, but I smiled at her and, since I was within reach, I took her hand, raised it to my lips.

Delicately, I kissed her hand and said, "My queen, let's go to our place. You have had me wanting for you all day. Thinking only of you, it is time you must fulfil your obligations." Her eyes glittered, the lust and violence were visible in her gaze. Dropping her head back while laughing out loud, she said the following. "My king, your wishes are my orders, I want to spend the whole day with you. Making up for lost time, your words have made me want you even more. What are we waiting for then?" We materialize in my catacombs, she went directly to my neck. But I stopped her by putting my hand in front of her. Her questioning face was comical.

I took her by the hand and led her to the pond. She placidly followed me, taking her to the centre. I stood in front of her. I took her jaw with my hand and kissed her passionately. Meanwhile, with my other hand below the surface. I began to accumulate energy, the water will cover it until it is time to release it. Concentrating the forces of darkness, a whirlwind of force began to generate. It was lethal. When the curse was ready, I abruptly released her. Pushing her back with such force that her body fell backwards onto the surface of the water. Making a large splash of water all around.

From where I was, I saw how she sank slowly, her eyes showed terror when she realized what was happening. Persephone's crown immediately flew into my hands. Denying being used by Drickblood. The vampire remained in the whirlwind of energy until she was stripped of all her powers and abilities. She was nothing anymore, just a disgusting demon traitor to her king. The same energy spits it out as if it was disgusted to have her. She ended up embedded in one of the walls, then fell to the ground without strength. Where she remained for a while until she could move again. She raised her face with a reproachful look, Ha! Funny that she feels betrayed, "Why my lord, tell me what have I done to make your anger settle on me?" I got out of the water calmly. Already outside, I directed my attention to the crown that I had in my hands. I watched her with purpose, it was a mistake to have crowned that demon. I took it with two hands and pushed it towards my chest, my body swallowed it, generating a flash of light.

When this crown sees the light again, it will be to adorn the head of the true Persephone, the chosen one, Moriah. Without paying attention to the demon lying on the floor, I let my body finish drying. When I turned to see her again, I could only feel hatred and revulsion towards her. I swore that she, and all those who betrayed me, will suffer unimaginable torture forever. I decided it was time, and walked over to where she was, my power circling around me ready to destroy. Drickblood scrambled to kneel before me, putting her forehead on the ground. Her body was visibly shaking, she was about to receive her final judgment.

I got close enough, my feet almost touched her head, then, I kicked her hard-throwing her across the room. Her body was at my mercy, powerless and with nothing. Her vampiric abilities were snatched away. The crown no longer provided her with power and protection, she was nothing.

I went to her again and said, "Drickblood, I'll tell you something, they, all your trusted ones, played you. All those who convinced you that you could deceive the king of the underworld. And come out victorious, they lied to you, they deceived you. You were vilely used, not even your clan leader and that heavenly envoy cares nothing about you." I paused for a second to see her reaction, and indeed she was so naive. Her pride did not let her see that she was an insignificant pawn in this war. Her eyes crystallized with fear, her blood began to flow from them. Oh! " Yes, Drickblood, I know everything. You were a very stupid demon, but that turned out well. Now I have a way to use you, to defeat my enemies, and you will do that for me, will you, Drickblood?"

I crouched down to her level and brought my face close to hers. Gifted her with a smile before stabbing my fingers into her abdomen. The vampire twisted in pain, the black liquid from her insides began to come out. And then I put my whole hand inside her cavity until I reached her core. She was panting by then.

Without wasting any more time, I ripped it from her body with a single blow. My hand was dripping with her blood and the core was still throbbing. I squeezed it with such force that it disintegrated in the air. Then I turned to see the vampire. I was so glad to see how hard it was for her to breathe. She put her hands around her neck and began to tear her own skin.

But it's not time to finish her off yet, so I formed a ball of energy and pushed it into her chest. With this, I will have total control, I will be able to see and hear everything. No one will suspect anything, since she is my puppet now. Drickblood took a breath of air and her life force returned to her body. Face down, she was panting incessantly. I'm glad to see her in pain. I grabbed her by the neck and lifted her into the air, she went limp, she didn't put up any resistance.

Holding her by the neck, I hit her against the wall. If I did not contain my anger, I would risk killing her. I threw her aside like a disease. Through my power, I created the chains that will be responsible for torturing her every day. I put a shackle around her neck and chained her to the ground. In the same way, she suggested for me to chain Moriah, she would crawl like an insect. It is now time for me to move on to my next step. No one will step foot here, ever again, as before. Thanks to her, this place ended up contaminated with demons of every kind. As I spit at her in the face, my rage resurfaced. I watched her crawl across the floor, I shoved her out of my way and disappeared.

I materialized in the throne chamber and invoked the presence of Thanatos. Likewise, I don't know what he's been doing since I gave him the order to eliminate the clan leaders. But it's better this way, things have changed and now, the game has new rules. In the midst of his powerful energy, Thanatos appeared. He bowed and raised his head, waiting for instructions. "Thanatos, the enemy is closer than we suspected. I'm afraid the heavens are involved, and they want to overthrow me. And I know I gave you an order before they put a curse on me, and I want to know what happened in the meantime." Thanatos nodded his head and said, "My king, I felt the angelic presence close by. But its power was masked, so it was difficult for me to identify it. Now you have confirmed my suspicions, the heavens have their spies infiltrating the kingdom. Not only are demons directly participating, but beings of light."

I nodded in understanding, but Thanatos continued. "I knew something was not right the last time I saw you, so I was alert and watched the clans more closely. I knew they were planning something when the queen was meeting with them more often than usual."

"There was a specific being that seemed suspicious to me. I knew that he was hiding his identity and that it was probably the being of light that you had detected. But

I put everything on pause until you managed to regain your senses. Although let me tell you, this time, it took you quite a while, my king."

ARRRGGH! "Silence, Thanatos! Those who conspire against me will pay dearly. What I didn't expect was the intervention of god. I never expected that they would wage war against me. Nathanael, Archangel Michael's envoy, helped form the curse. " I shook my head in frustration.

"My king, allow me to say something," I shook my head as a sign for him to continue. "We would have to face them."

Yes, we have to, "What I suggest, my king, is that you get proof of what they are doing, and/or witnesses."

"I imagine you are referring to Nathanael?" Thanatos nodded as if he knew what I was thinking. I already have an idea of what I am going to do if the heavens believed themselves so clever to conspire against me. I will be much more cunning to counterattack. My mind is already beginning to form a plan. I will force those from heaven to acknowledge the great mistake they have made. Thereby, winning some favours on them will be the way to go. And if they refuse, then I will have no choice but to declare war on them.

Chapter 5

The cave of the dragon
Moriah

When I opened my eyes, I did not know where I was. Everything around me looked so different from what I saw last time. But I have to be in the underworld, in hell. Because everything is macabre, and the smell is unbearable. Always smelling of rotten meat or death.

My body is not well, in fact, I have not been able to move since I woke up. At first, I was in and out of reality several times. I guess my mind wanted to be alert. But the damage that my body suffered is such, that it had no other choice than to remain unconscious trying to recover.

The little that I have observed about this place is that it is a cave. I am lying in a hole in the ground, nothing new. I have been living and sleeping on the ground for a long time now. But it is always difficult to know that I have been subjected to this inhumane treatment.

Inhuman, did I say it right? Sure, because. No! They are not humans, they are demons, dark beings from evil. Death is their table, betrayal, and mistreatment is the spoon with which they eat every day. I cannot overcome this. I refuse to think that I can get through this. A lot of pain and suffering has been thrown on my shoulders. Looking at myself here on the floor, unable to move. I don't know how I'm still breathing, I should have succumbed to death.

Everything would have ended if I had only had good luck on my side. But I can't escape life's insistence that I remain alive. I want to fly away from here, from the darkness, and from the smell of death. Just thinking consumes a lot of energy, and it is difficult for me to keep my eyes open for long. They always end up closing, and I do not know when I will open them again, just to face this reality again and again. And it is to wake up in this cave, with only my conscience alert, while my body sleeps.

****

My body doesn't react to anything. I don't know if I will ever be able to move, or if I will ever be able to do anything. As a result of this, even crying exhausts me, the pain in my soul is so strong, and I feel completely alone. Since I've been here, I've been alone, completely alone. I sometimes wonder whether I was hallucinating when I thought a black horse was approaching me in the last few minutes of my life. If that were true, I would have seen him by now, but no, nothing has changed. The situation I find myself in is alarming. And I have no idea what to do to end it. The time continues to pass, and sometimes, I think I felt something. I didn't want to get emotional, but maybe my finger moved, although I tried again, but in vain. I suspect it could just be my imagination because I want to be able to walk so much. That must have been the case.

The next time I woke up, I was sunk in misery and had no idea that I was yawning, shocking myself to realize this. As soon as I confirmed this was not an illusion or my imagination. My eyes filled with tears, and I did not stop crying. For it was an immense joy knowing that I could move something. Maybe tomorrow or the next day I could move something else.

The next time I noticed a change, it was my neck. I was uncontrollable and emotional. I tried to lean my head somewhere. It took me a lot of effort, but I finally succeeded. I used this opportunity to see around me. As I lifted my head a little, I noticed that I was lying on the ground, on the floor. Also, I managed to see my body, which is the least I should have done, as sadness went straight into my heart.

My body is covered in scars and marks of all sizes. My mind was forced to think back to all the torture I went through at the hands of those demons. The hateful faces, the insults, the provocation, the humiliations, it was all a lot. I needed to close my mind and not think about anything, but how do I do it if all I have is time and nothing to do? The resentment that was forming in me was sickening me. I did not want my existence to revolve around bad thoughts. But these marks, which are the witnesses and the proof of everything I suffered. They're not going to let me ever forget.

The next time I opened my eyes, I noticed that I didn't sleep so much. That I didn't go from consciousness to unconsciousness so often. Furthermore, my eyes have been open longer than closed, and my hands have become more motile. I can raise one arm for a few seconds.

In the time I spent thinking about what to do, my situation was quite precarious. I had no idea where I was, and I was always worried that those monsters would return to torture me. There was no doubt in my mind that they brought me here to heal. And that they would come back one day to continue the torture. What if they are telling the truth? That I am here for the sole purpose of getting pregnant? That is not possible, having a baby with an evil creature like them. My life won't be spent breeding disgusting creatures. I have to get out of here as soon as possible.

So, I made a plan. The first thing I had to do was regain mobility in my body. I began by working on my neck and my arms. I exercised the muscles to rebuild their strength. I practised several times a day, and when I felt another part of my body responding, I did the same. The training was hard, and my legs took the longest to improve, but I was almost there. After a few weeks, I was able to sit down, turn my head, move my neck, lift my arms, and regain strength in my legs. I was so proud of what I had done. For the first time since I opened my eyes here, I was able to stand up. My muscles protested, but I had to keep going. I practised walking around myself in the dark. I was very careful not to trip over anything and hurt myself. In that case, I continued with my exercise.

At the time, I was already in much better shape. It took a lot of effort to get to where I am today. But I believe that my body is strong enough to find a way out and escape this misery. The next time I awoke, I decided today was the day I would start exploring. Although, I always wondered why I was not hungry and why I was not cold. I remember when I was with the demons, hunger caused severe stomach cramps and more. As I got up, I walked farther and further away from the hole in the ground that is my bed.

After walking a few meters, I saw a small light tinkling in the distance. My heart began to race. I had to be very careful not to find anything. This place is full of evil and things that shouldn't exist.

With courage, I slowly walked to that place, my legs shaking from fear and anticipation. In all the time that I have been here, I have not seen or heard anyone. This is scary. The only things that I could find are those demons. If anyone sees me, it will be my end, of that, I am sure, but not before having fun with me as the others did. Following the steps with greater caution, I squatted down to the ground and crawled. I hoped that this would make me less visible, so I would run less risk of being seen. While crawling through the mud, my hands sank into it, as did my knees; the soil was wet and cold, as well as covered in moss. There were also pieces of bone, and there were a lot of them. This could be the burrow of some massive animal, as the remains appear quite old. But the light was getting closer and closer, I turned around looking everywhere. I had to be prepared if some creature suddenly appeared.

I got to a rock and I hid behind it, very cautiously. I poked my head to see what was ahead. My body froze to see what was in front of me. I tried to control my breathing since it was out of control. My eyes started to fill with tears. How can this be? It is my end, I will not be able to escape from this, a dragon, and it is huge! What I saw shining were his eyes. My hands were shaking, and my brain was unable to react. My consciousness returned after being petrified in the same place for a few seconds. And I was finally able to move. I slowly crouched down, not wanting to attract his attention.

I managed to completely hide behind the rock and leaned my back on it. Not only that, but I could not keep my breathing steady, my heart was filled with hopelessness. All I suffered and this would be my end, I would end up being eaten by that! Every time I closed my eyes, I saw him in my mind. He was a huge creature. His eyes shone like diamonds, his body seemed to have impenetrable armour. I could see his giant fangs coming out of his mouth. The lethal spikes poking out of his spine caused my brain to back out. It was something terrifying, and the remains that I saw on the floor were surely his preys.

But nothing hit me as hard as what I heard next, "Ah, I see that you are much better, human. It took you time to recover, those demons hurt you very badly this time." My face was completely paralysed, I could not even move my eyes. My pulse was about to explode from the amount of blood flooding my ears. My presence was known to that terrible beast. But the dragon spoke again, cutting off my thoughts, "Oh! I understand you are very, but very afraid of me. At the moment, you do not have to worry. I will not crush you with my feet or hit you with my tail until I pulverize your body. Or chew your soft body to swallow you whole. No, none of that. You can come out now."

What did he say? I can't even generate a word. Is he

threatening me, or is he playing with his food before eating it? I only know one thing, since I woke up in hell. I have only suffered at the hands of these creatures. And this dragon will not be the exception, but I cannot stay here, he already saw me, I have to take a risk. So, slowly I poked my head over the stone, the beast was in the same place, he hadn't moved. I got up with great fear and uncertainty, but I had to do it, there was no point in continuing hiding. I stayed behind the stone to protect myself anyway. I knew that if this animal wanted to hurt me, nothing would stand in his way.

As I waited for him to say something, honestly, I could not say a thing. Fortunately, this dragon had a lot to share with me, "How do you feel, human? When they brought you here, you were almost dead. Your body had suffered very heavy injuries, old ones and new ones. It is incredible how that stupid king of the underworld allowed something like this to happen." He waited for me to say something, but when he saw I was not going to open my mouth, he sighed and continued speaking. "I don't know why I'm helping him, it seems that he is not as bright as I expected, but anyway, let's move on to other topics." I stayed in the same place, just listening. Even though he told me that I had nothing to worry about. His mere presence and figure were enough for my brain to be very cautious.

"The king's Agalariept brought you here. I already told you that you came half dead. I don't know why he thought of bringing you to me. But the horse was quite convincing, I can tell you that." I saw the dragon get lost in his thoughts as if he was living that moment again. He shook his head and got back to reality. "As I was saying, he brought you here and forced me to keep you safe. Even from the king himself, that's why I insist that you should relax around me. If something happened to you, that would give me a lot of trouble with that demonic horse." He nodded his head and started walking towards me.

As I saw his immenseness closer and closer, the colour disappeared from my face. I remained in the same place without moving or making a sound. He was frightening from afar, and even closer. I closed my eyes, as I found it hard to watch him approach. Please don't hurt me, please, please, I thought to myself over and over. Even with my eyes closed, and motionless, the fear was eating me alive. I felt his breath hit my face. It was putrid and hot, it could kill me just by blowing on my face. When I managed to open them, the dragon was still in front of me. He made a small puff of smoke and said, "Wow! Humans, always so afraid, I'll let you walk through my cave. There's no way you can get out, in case you're thinking of finding an exit. And I'll tell you something too, in case you've wondered. My land has magical properties. This is what has helped you heal and has maintained your body without the need for food."

He shook his head up and down, "I was just saying." And with that done, he turned around and was lost in the dark. "Oh!" I couldn't believe it, I survived the encounter with a dragon. But now what do I do? He said there was no way out, so how can I leave before those demons come back for me? The only thing I can think of is to talk to him and try to convince him to let me go. Where? Although I'm not sure, it's better than waiting for them to decide my fate. And the most important thing is to avoid being used as a human incubator at all costs. I can't even imagine how such a thing could happen -- children are meant to be loved and to live as a family. Not to serve as weapons -- and neither will I.

I decided not to waste any more time and explore the cave, as the dragon called it. I needed to check for myself that there were no exits. Furthermore, I will also use the opportunity to exercise my body. As I need to be ready in case any chance to escape presents itself. As I walked through the cave, I checked each nook and cranny. But I have yet to find anything. Sadly, it seems the dragon told the truth, there is no way out of here. The only other option I have is to talk to this creature.

There must be something I can do to convince him to help me escape. So I plucked up my courage and went to the place where I first saw him. I was standing in front of the gigantic mouth of an entrance. The air that came from it was terrifying, it gave me goosebumps. My stomach was in knots, and my anxiety was very high. I couldn't help but shake in fear, so I took a deep breath and exhaled. The fear did not go away, but it gave me the pause to take the next step. After filling my lungs with air. I shouted with all my might "DRAGON," But nothing. I waited a little longer before calling him again, "DRAGON" This time, I didn't have to wait, as before. Because the dragon poked its head out, its snout was only inches from me.

Chapter 6

Nathanael
Narrator

As The Queen sat on her silver throne. She watched as the clan leaders took their place. At the semi-round table that was before her throne, and the throne of the king of the underworld. Completely in silence. The seven clans were meeting in the throne room to discuss the king's lack of cooperation. As well as the strategies they were using to overthrow him. The tension lingered in the room. While others were alert. Others were too excited to keep their objectivity. And others were filled with anxiety.

"My Queen, I'm afraid we have not achieved what we expected. Although you have kept him occupied while we moved our forces, I think it is not enough. You have to convince him more to accept our demands." Doomerth, the leader of the Doomind clan, said. As The Queen gazed at him apathetically, another clan leader spoke up. "Some of us suspect that the curse is fading away from the king. Several days ago, all these troubles with the king would not have occurred. His Majesty's thoughts used to revolve solely around you, but now they have shifted."

"I share your suspicions, Carldeath. I am sure that the power used by the celestial messenger was not enough to contain the all-supreme king of the underworld." Poissonaro, the leader of the Poissonarm clan, gave his opinion.

"Yes, clan leaders, we must increase the dose. But now it is very risky to meet with the divine messenger. Hence, one of us will need to go to heaven to meet with him. In the current situation, there is no point in taking risks because we are very close to obtaining the power. In my opinion, it should be brought up first with the celestial being."

"I am with you, Lothbark, the benign being will tell us the best path to follow. We will need all the help we can get. If the god of the underworld awakens, we will all be dead, unable to defend ourselves. Blooderek, leader of the Bloodrink clan, said, "We need to remain vigilant, we cannot let our guard down."

"Silence everyone," The Queen ordered, raising her voice. The clan leaders fixed their gazes on her as the throne chamber went silent. The Queen stepped down from her throne and walked towards them. After a few steps from the table, she paused and stared at them intently. "Demons of the underworld, yes, we need to enforce the curse, for the king has lost his initial fervour. The potion is weakening, so he is still in my possession, but I don't know how long he will be. Our knowledge of the king of the underworld is limited, as is our awareness of his power. "

While some clan leaders nodded in agreement, others

had worried looks on their faces. Nonetheless, The Queen added, "So we will, as the leader of the Lothbark clan suggested, but." The Queen paused, looking each of them in the eye. "The messenger from heaven must come to us." The clans' leaders started arguing among themselves, questioning The Queen's instructions.

There were some in favour and those who wanted to go directly to heaven. Yet, The Queen would have none of it, and in a darkened tone she said. "I assure you, it will be done as I have decided. He who comes from heaven will come to us." Turning around, the Queen walked up to her throne. Sitting down, she listened to the clan leaders' discussion. While they were busy, The Queen summoned her trusted advisor. It only took a few seconds for Headeath to appear out of nowhere.

Bowing to his Queen, he saluted her. Your servant is here to serve you." The Queen nodded and said, "Advisor, I have decided to summon the divine messenger. Everyone here is concerned that the curse we placed on the demon king is losing its effectiveness." It took the advisor a few seconds to think. He then said, "My Queen, I suggest sending a message explaining our issue to the divine envoy. I know they will know what to do. We have to wait for their response, and then we can move forward." She raised an eyebrow, considering that option. Throughout the chamber were also heard the murmurs of clan leaders. "Headeath, you are always so timely with your intervention. We will be implementing what you suggest. In the end, we risk everything; failure will not be an option."

The clan leaders nodded, they all agreed. The only thing left was to contact the heavenly messenger. The Queen threw her head back and rolled her eyes. She summoned the power of darkness. Seconds later, a portal formed in the middle of the chamber, and from the Queen's hand, a small white snake emerged.

This one went to the entrance of the portal, and crossed it. After this, the door closed immediately. No one can enter or leave the underworld without being detected. And this snake will notify the heavenly messenger of the demons' intentions. The only thing left to do is wait for the answer, and for it to arrive soon. The clan leaders and The Queen continued to discuss their strategies. They were greedily distributing the spoils, without even having it in their hands. The Queen was all bored watching them. But no one was aware that another force, even more powerful, was aware of what was happening.

The next point to be addressed left all the demons in the throne chamber silent. "My Queen, and the leaders of the clans, I have received reports that the human is no longer in the king's catacombs. After the lashing session, the human disappeared. No one knows where she is." The murmurs were immediate, the human was a fundamental part of their plans. It was essential that they had control over her. "Your Majesty, do you have any information on this?" The leader of the Bloodrink clan, Blooderek asked. The Queen was tapping her fingers on the armrest of the throne. When she heard this, she sat up straight and narrowed her puzzled eyes. And said, "The only thing the king of the underworld told me. It is that the human had been severely damaged after the lashing. And that he had to take her to someone who could fix her body."

She turned her attention to the adviser Headeath and

asked, "What else have you heard? And how is it that anyone knows that the human is no longer in the catacombs?" The demon adviser nodded his head and replied. "Your majesty, the human has been linked and marked by the tree of knowledge and the king's infernal steed.

Thus, everything that is directly linked to the king we will know. The curse that the celestial being conjures dictates the will of the king. That is why everything that happens to him, we will know. As long as the curse works." The Queen leaned back on her throne and said, "I see, if the king is having trouble with the curse, chances are the celestial being knows already. We will be hearing from him very soon if that is the case."

While all the demons present were giving their opinions and suggestions on how to do things. A flashing light appeared on the ceiling of the throne chamber. From that light, a figure of unique beauty emerged. His face seemed sculpted in the finest marble. His clothes were stitched with gold threads.

The being of light spread his imposing wings and descended to the floor. All the demons present gaped. And when they recovered from the shock, they bowed to the creature of light in reverence. Golden sparkles fluttered around his white hair. It was something incredible to witness. The beauty of the beings of light was supreme. The demons have always been envious of this. Being exiled to the underworld. Their bodies were transformed into repulsive and pestilential creatures. But there was only one demon who was watching all this with revulsion and excitement. He did not envy anything, because he had everything. The god of the underworld, the supreme Armaloth. He was waiting for exactly this moment, now, the positions of the game had changed, he had the upper hand.

The Queen immediately bowed before the being of light and said, "My Lord Nathanael, welcome. All of us were waiting to hear from you. Thank you for coming in such a short time." The being of light, Nathanael, observed each of the demons in the throne chamber. His beautiful honey-coloured eyes stopped on The Queen's adviser and said. "I received your message, my faithful Headeath. Your insight into detecting the problem was incomparable. And you will be rewarded with the favours of my Lord, the supreme Archangel Michael."

The demons around, including The Queen, began to wonder what was happening. But The Queen did not want to be left with doubt and asked the being of light, "What are you talking about? I was the one who sent you the message a few seconds ago." The clan leaders looked at each other, nodding their heads that it was true what the Queen was saying. The powerful angel turned to see The Queen, and his eyes flashed with intensity and purpose. He gave her a benevolent smile and shook his head with delicacy in disapproval. He raised an eyebrow and addressed The Queen, "King of the underworld, long time no see." Everyone present turned to see each other, asking what was happening. "We underestimated the power of the demonic triad. We knew that sooner or later you would awaken from the curse, but it was sooner than we had anticipated. Bad luck, that's all. I hope you are not offended, king of the underworld. My adored Lord only wants the best for everyone, no one can deny it."

The eyes were on The Queen. How was this possible, everyone wondered. Suddenly, the Queen froze. Like a statue, her eyes began to turn white, and they began to enlarge, more and more. Until the most feared creature of darkness emerged from them. His body radiated evil, injecting terror into the bodies of everyone present. The Queen fell to the ground, her body inert, seemed lifeless. The mighty Armaloth, yet, had other plans for her; he would not let her die so easily. Now that he had been discovered, he had no reason to remain in the shadows. Why not take advantage of this opportunity? Wondered the king.

The demons present could not believe what was happening before their eyes. Their lives were literally over, the collective terror began to be felt. Many fell to the ground as a sign of repentance. They could not do anything against the powerful god of the underworld. Armaloth didn't even pay attention to them, his full focus was on the divine being in front of him. The celestial being said, "Ah! There you are, king of the underworld. Thank you for joining us here."

Armaloth, the great king, smiled at the angel, saying, "Nathanael, I am surprised. That someone of Archangel Michael's ability. Could think that such a cheap trick could result in something effective. As you can see. You and your master are nothing compared to me. All you were very naive in thinking that something like this could harm me." The infernal king saw all the demons gathered in the throne chamber, and with a blink, they all fell to the ground. It seemed that their bodies were anchored to it. Having been discovered by the great king.

Some were sweating blood from anxiety and tension. Their bodies were about to explode.

After turning his back on them, the king of the underworld ascended to his throne. Sat on it, and immediately the thorny branches embraced him. Beside him, a black incandescent cloud began to form. And inside it, you could hear the neighing that could freeze anyone's blood by listening to it. The infernal steed of King Armaloth appeared in front of everyone. With a threatening look, of his eyes of fire, and without ceasing to neigh.

He stood on two legs, demonstrating his might, and his energy was deadly. Everyone was trembling at this. Even the celestial being doubted his abilities for a moment. The king's Agalariept stood guard to the right of his master. His thorny branches snake menacingly. There was an unspeakable malefic force radiating from the throne of thorns. There was no one who could defeat the dark lord.

And in front of the Lord of the underworld, a new cloud began to form. Thunder and lightning erupted from it, and its roars could shake anyone's soul. The divine being took a few steps back. His confidence was waning little by little. The tip of a scythe emerged from the thundercloud. It was the Lord of the dead. Suddenly, Thanatos appeared from the thunderclouds. His every step reverberated in the throne chamber. The day of judgment has finally arrived. The mighty god of death appeared dressed in black, with his deadly sword of death hanging from his belt. His wings spread wide. Acting as a protective shield between the incomparable Armaloth and the traitors. A scythe held high in his hand.

The throne chamber filled with such power was unimaginable. However, the king did not intend to destroy them. He had other plans. The celestial being, Nathanael, invoked the portal that would lead him to heaven. His only hope was to escape from there. So he knew he could never stand up to any of the dark beings in front of him, never mind both. The portal was present and open for him. With the power of the heavens, Nathanael was propelling himself upwards.

He reached the door but was immediately pulled back by the powerful forces of Thanatos. No one could escape them now. The mighty Armaloth, shook his head from side to side, disapproving of this action. Then he smirked. "Tsk, tsk, No! Nathanael, none of that, I have not dismissed you." In an attempt to break free from the power that held him to the ground, the being of light struggled. It was impossible for him to match the real strength of the underworld; he was no match for it. Before his power was taken, the being of light managed to send a message to his lord, the Angel Michael.

Thanatos was given the go-ahead by Armaloth to carry out the plan. Suddenly, the god of death waved his scythe of evil. As a result, an energy current circulates through the chamber. With such amazing power, a whirlwind was created. It swallowed all the unfortunate creatures who had gathered to defeat Armaloth. Whirlwinds grew smaller and smaller.

Until it fits in the palm of the terrible Thanatos' hand, then solidified into a crystal sphere. The Lord of Death managed to contain all the demons and the angelic being in that place. Thanatos saw the angelic being banging on the glass walls. Then he handed the sphere to his lord, the god of the underworld. After watching them for a moment, he laughed out loud with a malevolent grin.

Chapter 7

Archangel Michael
Armaloth

As I sat on my throne, I marvelled at the crystal sphere that held my enemies. I finally managed to get rid of these parasitic demons. I extended my arm while holding the crystal sphere in my hand. Suddenly it levitated and then disappeared in a loud explosion of sparkles. For now, it'll stay in the damned dimension. "Thanatos, I have decided to act as soon as possible. I am not sure how much information Nathanael was able to pass on to his master. Besides, I don't believe they are expecting us so soon. My Alastors' army must be ready, too. The horsemen must be involved in this as well, but I'll be the one dealing with them."

Thanatos nodded in acceptance as he awaited more details. "You will be responsible for preparing everything. We will go to heaven once everything is ready, and I have a lot to say to that Archangel. I want to know if he has the support of his god, or is it an independent attack. First, have a demon from each clan brought to me as soon as possible. It is time to name the successors. We need to have the support of all clans in the event that war cannot be avoided." The god of death bows and disappears. The thorny branches snaked around me as I stood up from my throne. My arms spread wide as I rolled my eyes. The energy of destruction should be concentrated. I opened my third eye and emitted a beam of light that transcended dimensions.

The lightning bolt returned as well as the four horsemen of the apocalypse. The rider of death materialized first in front of me on his yellow Agalariept. Having emerged from the thick cloud of smoke with his scythe in hand, holding it high. And a human skull adorned his head. He wore a necklace made of humans skulls too on his chest. Death and destruction flashed in his eyes. Immediately behind him, the mighty Hunger Rider emerged, astride his black Agalariept. The body of this monster had skin stuck to the bones.

His face looked like a charred human face. A whip tangled around the neck of this powerful immortal. Those who had a braver heart would have been terrified by the vision. And now, it was time for the War Immortal to appear, riding his majestic Agalariept. He carried his sword on his back, still dripping with blood from his enemies. The helmet on his head was topped with twisted dragon horns. And the armour he wore was made from the dragon's impenetrable scales. This appears to be his latest victim.

And finally, the immortal that you least want to meet on your way. Known as Pestilence, he has the ability to rot everything in his path, and his mere presence can cause death. His appearance is repulsive, his skin looks like it is flaking off. The white Agalariept that accompanies him is just as disgusting. My four horsemen were finally in front of me. They dismounted from their horses and bowed to me. One by one, they rose to their feet and swore allegiance to the supreme king of the underworld. Nodding my agreement, I began, "The heavens are interfering with our affairs. I have captured their spy. Along with the former queen. He led a group of treacherous demons calling itself the council of seven. They are conspiring to overthrow me."

My blood began to boil just thinking about that. "Archangel Michael is behind all this. But I don't know for sure who else is involved. However, it would be foolish of him to do it alone. It is for this reason that I summoned you." They nodded their heads in agreement, understanding what was going on. "King of the underworld. Based on what I understand and have heard, the heavens do not want you to form your army with the women."

"These beings of light are not allowed to harm humans due to their sanctity. It's for this reason that they're messing with us." It was an apt comment from the war horseman. "The best course of action is to attack us. Set up a rebellion within the underworld and allow the same demons to eliminate the human." I nodded my head in agreement. "The dragon demon warned me about all this, but I am not sure where he stands in all of this. Essentially, what he told me was that he had nothing better to do. Are there any of you who know anything? This time, it was Pestilence who replied. "Mighty king, the dragon will not accept, for any reason, that the heavens have an advantage over the demons. It doesn't matter what the posture of the great beast may be right now, simply he won't stand with the heavens ever."

"Mm, yes! That makes sense, and it reassures me. I don't want to have to face the legendary dragon for any reason." It was at that moment that Thanatos manifested. Having noticed the cloud in the centre of the throne room, we all turned our attention to it. The demon Thanatos, along with seven others, emerged from it. There is no question that these are the ones that will replace the traitors. The seven demons knelt down and touched their foreheads to the ground.

All of them remained in the same position until I told them to get up. "I have summoned you here, demons from all clans, as your leaders have been accused of treason." There was an exchange of glances between the demons. Then one of them knelt down and touched the ground with his forehead. "Great underworld king, master, and lord. We don't know about that, if we had, we would have come directly to you."

He was sweating profusely, and I could hear his teeth clenching with nervousness. The other demons nodded their heads in agreement with what the demon had said. In order to end their suffering, I said, "You have been chosen. You will be the next clan leader. The responsibility of guiding your demons is upon you all. Then, pledging allegiance to me and my kingdom."

In front of me, the demons swore obedience and loyalty to my reign. The next step was to prepare them for the impending war. "Thanatos will tell you what to do, so you can leave now." My attention now turned to Thanatos after the demons were gone. "Whenever you are ready." After Thanatos agreed, he swung his scythe. And a portal filled with glowing energy appeared before us. The glowing skull heads of my impressive and magnificent army of Alastors were there. They are ready for battle inside the portal. Stepping in, my body felt as if it were being absorbed.

****

After coming out of the portal, my foot touched enemy soil, and my army followed behind me. After just arriving, my stomach was already turning. The last time I was here, it was when we were banished to the underworld. The place has become more and more unsightly over the years. I do not remember it being this bad before. The air here is so pure that it is hard for me to breathe. Stepping into this place is like stepping into a war zone. And to return to my darkness, I already wish to end this. As I looked at my demons, they did not seem to be enjoying themselves, they appeared to be suffering from a clear blow. I gestured to Thanatos with my head to move. When in the distance, the entire horizon appeared to glow.

I stopped and ordered everyone to do the same. The angelic forces already knew we had arrived. And they are here to welcome us. I took the reins of my Agalariept and rode it. Together we are invincible. So I wait in that same place for the divine envoys to approach. In the distance, I could already see their silhouettes more clearly. My army was eager to attack, as these beings of light approached, I could now be able to see their faces. It was a fairly powerful contingent, it was made up of most of the enforcers. Both in heaven and on earth, they are responsible for maintaining order.

Among the rest, there were angel soldiers. So perhaps. My presence wasn't interesting enough for any higher-ranking divine being to acknowledge me. Those obnoxious winged beings. Those despicable archangels knew what they were doing, but I have no interest in playing their games.

Deadly energy began to emanate from my hands. The power of the underworld is unsurpassed. Even God himself would not be so foolish as to face me directly. From my hands, energy began to radiate all around me; my demons became immersed in it. And I felt their strength multiply. Suddenly, the crystallized ground we were standing on began to turn necrotic. The angelic contingent immediately stopped. And among them, an old acquaintance whom I had never expected to see again emerged. He took a few steps forward, and I had to decrease the intensity of my energy. He watched my army and then, he paid special attention to the horsemen of the apocalypse. They should be on the heavenly side, not mine, but some circumstances have put them in my path. "Armaloth, my friend, it has been a long time without you being around."

"I heard you will be here in heaven, with us, for a visit, so I thought to enjoy your presence. What has life been like for you so far? Azrael smiled sincerely as he greeted me. Unfortunately, our story ended the moment I was banished to the underworld. But that's no reason to be rude to him. After all, he and I were always the best team around. "Azrael, my old friend, yes, it has been a long time since we saw each other." I watched him, assessing his power and ability. Yes, Azrael is lethal, in fact, one of the best in battle, and maybe he has even improved over time.

"Unfortunately this is not a social visit. I have some business to resolve with the unscrupulous Archangel Michael." Azrael raised an eyebrow upon hearing me say this. I don't know how much he knows about this, but he's not my target. "Yes, I heard something like that. I am not here for anything other than to greet you, our past deserves a little respect and for my part it has it." That's right, the Azrael I know has always been a faithful angel. "Always so true my friend. But this matter is not easy. If I came here, it means that something serious is going to happen."

"With the darkness at my side, I have an infinite amount of power; not even your own god can directly stand in my way. That's why he had to resort to these cheap tricks." But Azrael just looked at me without expression. "You are a warrior of the heavens, and you will do whatever it takes to fulfil your responsibility."

"But for the sake of all you, I hope your leaders heed my demands." Azrael nodded, understanding the dilemma. And he said "Unfortunately for us, my friend, my god comes first of all. I will remain faithful to him, but I will not stop caring about you, Armaloth." I nodded my head in acceptance of his sincerity. There are few people who can provide that. "I must speak to that cheater, Miguel. Tell him that if he doesn't come to me in less than an hour, the underworld will declare war on your god." The statement surprised my old friend, but that's how it is. He then stepped back and nodded. Yet, he left a contingent of Angels watching us.

****

This place, the heavens, made me realize that it had been so long since I had been on this plane of existence. Here are my origins, my being was created from the life force of this place. Maintained by the pure and immaculate energy of the god.

Everything is pure, there is nothing hidden, broken or corrupted here. You can be filled with energy without being damaged by it. You are restored, purified, and soothed, rather than the other way around. Quite the opposite of my world, strangers cannot live there. You will be destroyed by the underworld's energy in a matter of seconds. Everything good will become bad. Everything healthy will become ill, everything beautiful will become ugly. My world is there, and I am not in a good mood being here. I can't help but think that somehow this place was etched into my mind. We have so much history together that it will be impossible to forget it. There hasn't been any change here; the floor is still crystalline, soft, and warm to the touch. There is a feeling that I am walking in sand made of crystal dust. No clouds are in the sky, always resplendent. Anything you hide here will be exposed. Neither have the celestial warriors moved from their vantage point. Nor have they turned their gaze away. How would they react if I decided to attack them? My power is unlimited, these poor winged will disintegrate in an instant. They were left here for appearances' sake because they can't fight me. I don't know why, it is pointless. The heavens are losing their touch, poor deluded, winged, holy beings.

Suddenly, I was warned of many approaching entities by my Agalariept. Finally, the naive one who thought he could challenge my kingdom. In the distance, four figures can be seen. It was easy to recognize him from centuries ago. In all his glory, Michael the Archangel rests under the protection of his god. Despite all the time since I last saw him, his beauty has not faded, but I cannot say that the same would be true for me. As a result of being consumed by darkness, my entire being is dark now. It does not apply to him, he still ranks among the best.

Anyone who sees his long, red hair is always amazed at how beautiful he looks, for God made him that way. As are his green eyes, as if they were the very essence of nature itself. He looks dangerous with his muscular body and lean frame. My knowledge of him is superior to anyone else's, and I know he is dangerous and potentially deadly. A celestial being of the highest order, he is one of God's creations. A stunning figure with skin that glows as if it were made from pure crystal, he is quite beautiful. Possessing a placid demeanour all the time. The next one in command is Gabriel. The fact that he always does the dirty work shows his ability to solve problems at the slightest effort. Recruiting him into my ranks would make us invincible. He is the most cunning of all, he can entangle you without you even realizing it.

Even though he is not as tall as Miguel, he has a powerful, indestructible body.

The holiness of his life makes him in tune with the energy that surrounds this place. God's power protects him from all harm. If I were to defeat him, I wouldn't know how long it would take. That's how incomparable he is. The other figure is none other than the mighty Uriel. Purifying demonic energy and turning it into pure energy is one of his specialities. There would be no demon who would want to bump into him. Like all of them, their beauty is admirable.

The golden threads in his hair look like they are made of gold. I have never seen such enormous wings, and as they unfold, they captivate everyone who sees them. They are made of small segments of crystals, impenetrable and lethal when they attack you. And of course, Azrael, my old friend. His loyalty will always go to his god, despite our past. His loyalty is unquestionable. Because he discovered Lucifer's plan and informed the god himself. And the heavenly armies of our brewing betrayal. He can see right through the obvious, into the most intimate secrets and the most well-kept lies, he knows it all. Standing in front of me were four heavenly archangels. My horsemen flanked me and my loyal steed was always at my right side. Now is the time to take control.

Chapter 8

The pact with the dragon
Moriah

I was struck by the dragon's massive gleaming eyes as soon as I saw him. I took a few steps back, even though I was more determined than ever to face him. I still felt threatened by his mere presence. As the dragon approached me, I had to jerk my head back as he became closer and closer. He was a monster, and so near to me. Smoke flowed from the dragon's nose as he yawned loudly. I felt his foul breath hit me in the face. The dragon blinked several times to adjust his gaze until it settled on me. "I thought it was a dream. I had already forgotten that you were around here, this head of mine." The dragon shook its head and then sat up. "What can I do for you, Queen of the underworld?"

I denied with my head, the title with which he referred to me, and said "Dragon since I woke up in the underworld. I have not stopped suffering. I know that you do not care about my life, or what happens to me. Although we are strangers, I am sure there is a way for you to help me." Apparently, the dragon thought I had lost my mind as he gazed at me. That's how I felt. All this was beyond my comprehension. "In what way can I help the Queen of the underworld?" I took a deep breath in order to calm down how exasperated I was at this moment. "Dragon, I am not the Queen of nothing. My name is Moriah, I think. But the important thing is that you tell me how to get out of here."

Several seconds later, the dragon laughed aloud. I couldn't understand what it was that amused him so much. The dragon, despite its intimidating size, was a bit annoying. Having laughed as much as he wanted, he said, "Moriah, right," I nodded my head in agreement and continued. "Where do you want to go, so the demons can't find you?" I was afraid to hear that, my eyes would pop out of my sockets.

Having reflected on what he said, I replied: "Dragon, I don't know anything. The only thing I know about myself is that nobody has told me anything about myself. The only thing I know is that filthy demon Armaloth has me here to torture me. Also, let's not forget that they want to use me to power an army with their own children." That's completely ridiculous. "Help me, dragon, I know there is something that I can do for you." I searched his eyes, with passion and hope in my heart.

Yet, the dragon was not at all convinced. Please dragon, what are you going to lose?" The dragon shook his head several times before telling me, "You said you knew nothing. That's the same as throwing a baby out on the street. You are like that little baby, defenceless and ignorant." Despite the fact that he said the truth, his words still hurt. But, I would rather go to any other destination, those that the demons have in mind for me.

"Dragon, it doesn't matter, anywhere is better than here, no offence intended. However, I will not be able to live where there are demons. My refusal is to play by their rules. I need guidance, so please tell me something." The dragon was thinking, considering what he wanted to say. "I don't intend to commit to anything with you, but I'd like you to see something. You say you don't know where you're from? Well, I'll show you. Once you've seen this, you'll tell me what you'd like to do." After swallowing with worry, I nodded my head in agreement. Finally, knowing where I had come from and what I was doing before appearing here. As he began walking, I stood aside quickly, allowing him to exit from his cave, without stamping on me.

Turning to face me, he threw his head back. The ray of light that came from his mouth radiated throughout the cave. As the light spread, I began to see images that I had never seen before. People and places are totally different from where I was now. And they were like me; I saw small creatures walking alongside humans. It was a beautiful place, there were trees, plants, and lakes. There was no way I could blink for fear of missing something. That's the world I come from, and it's beautiful. The images suddenly changed, and a man was holding a little baby girl in his arms. The man appeared to be happy.

The baby was smiling, drool dripping from her chin, but she didn't care. The man grabbed the baby and held her in his arms. The baby couldn't stop laughing, she was happy just being in the man's arms. In a moment, the wonderful image changed, and she became a girl playing in the park. She was accompanied by the same man, who simply watched her play. Suddenly, another image appeared. Both were standing on sand, and around them was a vast body of water, deep blue, where you could see there was only water. She held the man's hand, and they walked along the shore together. From time to time, the girl collects things from the sand. While she carried a small container. She watched with fascination the things she was placing inside.

A new set of images appeared, and the same girl was with the same man, but in a different location. Time passed, and the girl became taller and more intelligent. She studied a lot, you could tell she loved books. It was always her and the man, people came and went, but they never separated, they remained together. I felt like my heart was cramping watching them for some reason. There was something missing, and I didn't know what it was.

The more I watched, the more tears filled my eyes, and the more my heart longed for them. The one that used to be a girl, was no longer one, the following images were of her in a university. I saw that she was admired by many, as well as many seeking her help. Among all of them, she was the most knowledgeable. The man was always proud of who she was, and was always by her side, helping her in everything.

A part of me opened up as if the images had provided the answer to what I didn't realize I was seeking. At that moment, I knew it was me, and the man always by my side was my father. I covered my face with my hands and dropped to the floor on my knees. The pain in my heart was unbearable. My father. I remember everything now, thousands of memories have flooded my mind.

After being kidnapped, I was able to remember everything from my past. Now I knew who I was. My name is Moriah Regina, and I am a prodigy in psychiatry. Daughter of one of the most prestigious doctors of the 20th century. I lay on the floor sobbing. What I discovered today was something that completely unsettled me. Now I had a reason to move on, my father, my life. That is why I will get out of here and fight for what is mine.

After spilling the last drop, I wiped my face with my hand and stood up. I was now faced with the dragon demon. When I looked straight at him, only determination could be seen in my eyes. I said, "Dragon, it's time to go home, and I expect you to help me. You will help me if you consider me the queen of the underworld." Although the dragon narrowed his fierce eyes, I was determined. I held his gaze until he finally answered me. "So now you're the queen of the underworld, uh? That changes everything." Hearing that made my stomach churn with anxiety. My being was filled with hope. Please, please, please, I begged in my mind. But I was surprised at the dragon's next words. "It is true that you are The Queen of the underworld, chosen by the tree of knowledge and the king's Agalariept."

Then he nodded to himself, confirming what he said. "You are the queen, yes. Yet, the king will not let you go so easily, actually, he won't let you go at all. He will search for you in all the worlds, and he will find you. Where you hide doesn't matter."

All the hopes that had flooded my heart will disappear, leaving me empty. It can't be this, it has to be something else. I only have one option and that is to find an alternative. "Help me, if I cannot do it forever. Then, please give me some time, whatever it takes, but I want to stay with my father as long as possible." My father is the only thing that matters to me now. This was the first time I had seen him this way; he was always by my side. All the time, until the last moment, his life is dedicated to me. After carefully observing me, the dragon demon sighed heavily and said to me:

"Moria, I will help you return to your world, but it won't last forever. The King of the underworld is very powerful. I could say he is even more powerful than I am. Although I have nothing to fight for, he does, so you can be sure he will do everything in his power to reach you." Still, I just shook my head in acceptance. Once again, I had to beg him "Please dragon, please help me. Help me, just for a little while." The dragon watched me, his eyes shining with intensity. "What would you give me if I helped you?" Oh! That caught me off guard, so I replied, "What could a dragon like you want?" The dragon began laughing.

He always does the same thing. "Oh, there's one thing I want. Upon returning, I will spend time with you. " That made my whole face light up with a smile. The cheeky dragon that he is. This is the first time I've smiled since I woke up in the underworld. "Done, dragon." The dragon nodded and said, "Done, Moriah of Armaloth." After this, he blew a puff on my face and my body began to fade. As I stared at him in uncertainty, my entire being seemed to disappear, and the last thing I heard was the dragon's voice telling me the follow: "Your father's last day on earth will be the day the king comes for you. Not one day more, not one day less. Moriah, queen of the underworld,

I look forward to seeing you again. " That was the last I heard of the dragon before the darkness took hold of me.

****

My eyes opened with difficulty. The bright light hitting my face made this task difficult. As soon as I managed to open them, I was greeted with the most beautiful image I'd ever seen. That afternoon I cried as I had never cried before. I was in my world. After I awoke, I found myself in the same place where I had been abducted by Armaloth.

Looking around, I slowly got up to see the beautiful vineyards of Monsieur Aubèrt. Now that there was no one with me, I was absolutely sure I was alone. There were no shadows, no presences, and no Armaloth to be found. While looking down, I noticed that I was wearing clothes. The outfit I wore that fateful day is still fresh in my memory. I found it incredible. That, in the underworld, I never put anything on myself, and I never felt ashamed. And I was not aware of my nakedness. But here, I'm so happy to be wearing these clothes. With so much longing, I hug my body. This was something that I missed so much, I couldn't imagine doing anything else. My shoes caught my attention as I looked below. My mind could not escape remembering how I walked like an animal, hands and feet always filthy. I had no dignity, but the abuse had ended, so at least for now, I'm safe.

As I walked to the exit of the arena, I noticed that the altar and the dagger were missing. I paid no more attention to that. And turned around, turning my back to everything. After rushing to the exit, I ran as hard as I could; I didn't want to be without my father any longer. Only he was on my mind, to see him, to hug him. I will not stop telling him how much I love him and how grateful I am for everything he's done for me throughout his life. I ran straight through the vineyards without stopping. Not only that, but I was excited, probably soaked in sweat, but nothing mattered anymore. I understood the true meaning of life. I will put the most important thing at the top.

The more steps I took, the closer I got to home, I crossed the garden, until I reached where the party was being held. I stopped at the entrance to look around. There were a lot of people in the place. Nothing else, the shadows had disappeared. It was finally over for me. As I walked forward, I wiped away the tears that had been shed. I immediately focused my attention on the person who I was most interested in seeing. Then I spotted him, he was chatting with one of his friends. My mind suddenly triggers all kinds of memories. Out of nowhere, I see myself as a different person. I was complete.

I stayed in the same place and watched him from afar. When he saw me, he shook his head, letting me know that he was keeping an eye on me. I smiled at him as I had never done before, and joined the party. Then I grab a glass of wine that one of the waiters carried on their tray and enjoy the first sip. By the time I finished my glass of wine, I was calm and confident enough to begin chatting with others. After interacting with humans for quite some time, I went to see my father. For a while, I watched him and saw that he was filled with a love I had never before seen.

As I embraced him, I felt his warmth radiating through my skin. His hug was so warm, and I felt so protected like he was the hero of my childhood. My eyes were red after we finished hugging. Having just woken up, it has been impossible to stop crying. "Is everything okay with you, Moriah? Did anything happen? If you don't feel OK, we can go, and you won't have to deal with the emotions that may trigger something." I nodded, and with that, we started saying goodbye to everyone. It was a very pleasant afternoon, and one I will never forget.

I had been thinking about the French countryside. Marvelling at the beauty of its landscape. The road was silent, I was contemplating the scenery. And after spending so much time in the underworld. Never again will I take my freedom for granted. And I think about moving here, with my father. Will be the best decision ever. When we got to the house, I got out of the car and looked around, everything was the same. What surprised me the most is that I spent a horrendous amount of time in that place. Then, we went into the house and the first thing my father did was ask me what was wrong with me.

"Moriah, I think the medicine is affecting your emotions, if this continues, we will have to review the dose and adjust the toxicity levels and..." I didn't give him time to finish. "Don't worry, I'm okay, Dad. There were no side effects from the medicine. There is no reason for me to fear it failing. "

"I can tell you with certainty that we have found a new cure. We have developed a new medicine, do you know what that means? We will go down in history together. My father looked at me suspiciously, but when he saw my enthusiasm, he relaxed and gave me a shy smile. He chuckles, but till this moment, I didn't realize how beautiful he looks when he smiles. "What can I expect, my daughter is a genius." My father said he couldn't help himself.

Chapter 9

The Confrontation

The king's Agalariept was nervous. Shifting from side to side, shaking his head at the threat before them. His thorny branches, always on guard. Both he and his master were ready. Besides, the lord of evil had his horsemen and many demons and Alastors at his disposal.

Before the king, the Archangels were expectant. Now, what will the king of the underworld do? Then they wondered. "Archangel Michael, you honour me with your presence. I thought you wouldn't come to greet me." The archangel looked at him coldly. "That is what I have been wondering about, Armaloth. The dark king would have a reason for being here, wouldn't he? Coming to the holy land? You may say what you wish to say and then leave. You are disturbing the peace of this sanctuary with your presence. Please do not take this the wrong way. "

"I see! I didn't know you held me in such high regard, Miguel." The two opponents stood face-to-face. Although neither of them wanted to give in, Armaloth was here for a reason. Without further ado. He extended his palm in front of him. And the crystal sphere containing the traitors materialized in front of everyone. With a CLUNK, the king of the underworld crushed it and the demons and holy creature fell to the ground. Their eyes were fixed on them. As the Archangel, Michael surveyed the scene. His furious gaze was directed towards Armaloth. His dark nemesis also watched him, waiting.

The Archangel Michael walked toward where Nathanael was. He never looked away from his heavenly servant. Power and superiority were evident in his steps. There was no one who dared to stand in his way. When he reached his faithful servant. He bent down and touched with the tips of his fingers, his servant's bruised and dirty cheek. From Nathanael's eyes, tears began to flow. The mighty Archangel wiped them away and smiled at him. Then picked up Nathanael in his arms and carried him like a baby. The heavenly servant hid his face in the neck of his master. Absorbing his energy and bathing in his presence. Nathanael was now at peace, safe in the arms of his beloved teacher and mentor. The mighty Archangel went with the other angels. Concern filled all their hearts for their angelic disciple, Nathanael.

The incomparable Archangel rested his chin on the head of his beloved disciple for the last time. Showing him all his love and support. Before giving it to his brother, Uriel. Immediately after receiving him in his arms, he then turned his gaze toward Miguel, for a short moment. Uriel shook his head as a sign that he understood what to do. The mighty, miraculous Archangel generated energy around himself. There was something so bright and warm about this energy. It was like the embrace of salvation. So much so that all the demons present were trembling in fear. They had to avoid being touched by this pure energy at all costs.

The beings of darkness stepped back. Far from him. Those who couldn't escape in time were enveloped in this incredible energy. In the face of the power of heaven, they were helpless. Suddenly, the energy started to work. With this light, the lost and damned demons were filled one by one. Where the energy was going, a trail was left. Gradually, hatred gave way to love, anxiety to peace, and pain to wellness.

The faces of those demons captured by darkness now showed serenity. The Archangel Uriel had the power to destroy the same demonic marrow. End evil. There was nothing more terrifying than Uriah. As his light touched them, all the demons began to crystallize. Their bodies were transformed into crystal statues. This caused the other demons to flinch. Seeking refuge behind his master and lord Armaloth.

The king of the underworld stood in the same place. His evil energy was so strong that even those little flashes of angelic energy were unable to harm him. Even so, he refused to expose himself, so he formed a protective shield in front of him. This would contain the purification of light emanating from the magnificent Archangel. The great demon saw his demons crystallizing. Even the bravest of them were shaken by what happened next. The crystal statues exploded into a thousand pieces. Creating a sparkling cloud around them. Their heads were covered in crystal dust. Armaloth did not take his eyes off him, He had to be careful with this Archangel. Because his purifying energy was so powerful. That even he could run the risk of being affected. That truth made him temper with resentment and hatred towards the beings of light.

Archangel Uriel. On the other hand, continued to radiate his benign energy. Nathanael was engulfed by it. The body, completely devoid of light, gradually began to be possessed by the spirit of the divine. His dry guts were once again at peace. His fractured bones began to heal. And his spirit became stronger, despite having been tortured and dejected. While he was locked in the demonic dimension. He was being corrupted, and his body deteriorated. His angelic being had been poisoned, hurt, and weakened. The darkness was consuming him.

The powerful Archangel Uriel closed his eyes. And his energy stopped emanating from his being. Then he carefully lowered Nathanael to the ground. In a gesture of gratitude and respect, he kissed his hand and bowed his head. Afterwards, he turned to his teacher Miguel and went to him. Being a few centimetres away. Nathanael leaned before his master and touched his feet with his forehead. The mighty archangel just smiled, and said: "My faithful Nathanael, get up." The grateful angel did that. Face to face, they embraced. Nathanael leaned his head against his master's chest. And let himself be enveloped in his essence. His love was unconditional. With envy, the demons present viewed this exchange of love and gratitude. They are aware that they will never have this relationship with their master and lord. It was even less likely that the dark Lord would shed a tear for them. Armaloth is consumed by darkness, and so are they all.

At the end of their embrace. The Archangel Michael indicated to his beloved servant to move behind him. And he did it without thinking. As the light beings turned their attention to the demons, their expressions hardened. They had harmed one of his brothers. "Archangel Michael, that angel, has been found in my kingdom. However, that was not all. He was with all these miserable traitors. Planning my downfall. " The mighty king points to the demons that were on the ground. The queen and the seven clan leaders and the advisor were cowering. On their knees, incessantly asking for forgiveness.

"What reason do they have for wanting to do away with you, dark lord?" With an intrigued expression, the great archangel replied. But the dark Lord laughed out loud, threw his head back. "Why? You ask me why, Miguel? I'm going to answer you why. For power, that's all we all want, power."

"Your angel and that demon there." Armaloth points at the former Queen Drickblood. "They cursed me to manipulate me and get what they wanted. That is what your heavenly messenger does. What I can't understand is how you could even think of stopping me with that little trick."

Darkness emanated from the evil being. And ferociousness increased as he remembered what had happened. There was no way to mock the black lord without dying. There is nobody. The mighty Archangel thought for a moment. And without taking his eyes off Armaloth, he then said in a soft and gentle tone, "Explain to me." Behind him, his servant Nathanael stepped forward. He clung to his master's side and replied, "My beloved master. It is true what the king of the underworld says. "

The heavenly being Miguel shuddered within, but he never showed it. His face was always steady. On the faces of the other Archangels as well, there was no expression. Moreover, they were concerned about what this immature messenger brought upon himself. "Master, you should know why I did it," He replied. Miguel nodded his head. Giving him permission to continue. "I was in the field of wishes. Collecting the following miracles to perform for our followers on earth. Among what I saw, one caught my attention. This desire was so bright and full of pain that I was immediately drawn to it."

"The message stated clearly and without elaboration, *"Please save my daughter. Angels of heaven save her."* When I touched the wish, my heart was filled with suffering and pain. This person had conveyed his feelings in such a way. That the fervent desire to protect his daughter took root in me. So I collected the wish along with others, as I always do."

"That afternoon, I started working on them. And when it was the turn of this wish, I discovered that it was from the faithful Philip Regina. The father of Moriah Regina, the one chosen by the Tree of Knowledge and the Hell King's Agalariept."

Armaloth's eyes grew wide. In the centuries of his life, he would never have thought this would happen. It was the father of his wife who sent the beings of light to help her. This had nothing to do with power and glory. But with fulfilling one of the divine commands to help souls in distress. The angel Nathanael acted completely selfless in this act.

"Since I was not able to deny him our help due to my spirituality, so I made a plan for her. According to what I saw, everything went according to plan. She is fine now." The angelic being moved his beautiful honey-coloured eyes towards his teacher and said. "Forgive me, my graceful lord. I didn't tell you anything, because I didn't want you to get involved."

"It was better for your faithful servant to bear the responsibility and punishment. I wasn't going to let you get involved, master. I love you so much that I will give up everything for your safety. However, I could not let go of this wish. He got hold of me in a way that I couldn't let it go. I'm sorry master, forgive me."

Finally, the stoic face of Archangel Michael turned into one of surprise. It was hard to keep it up. And surprisingly, the mighty Michael embraced his servant Nathanael. As the other Archangels approached, they hugged each other. The beings of light exuded such strong emotion that it was a sight to see. Demons were also touched by this. Perhaps the fact that they were in heaven was affecting them. The Beings of Light finally finished the hug. And Mighty Michael smiled warmly at his disciple, saying, "Silly Nathanael. You are my beloved brother and disciple. I love you just as much as you love me. There was no other choice for you, I understand that. Your spiritual being had to respond to the supplication of the faithful follower. "

"You did it yourself so as not to put me in danger and avoid a confrontation with higher powers. By putting your life at risk. Nathanael, you are brave, my beloved."

After looking at his heavenly brothers, the Archangel nodded his head. They agreed on the next steps to be taken. "King of the underworld, my servant had no choice. So are the rules in heaven, and you know it. We place the lives and souls of humans above all else. There is no reason for you to attack him. I think the time Nathanael spent in that horrible dimension was enough punishment for him in any case."

"Now I suggest you restore order in your kingdom. Your house is dirty, and it needs to be cleaned. Go in peace with the grace of god, Armaloth, king of the underworld. "

Armeloth was speechless. His mouth fell open. It all made no sense. The father of his chosen one was the culprit of all this. Armaloth also understood that the heavens were within his right to assist souls in need. He was also subject to this, the heavens had agreed to it with Lucifer. This will maintain order. Armaloth was filled with resentment and helplessness. He generated a portal that would lead to his kingdom. All of his demons were absorbed by the hurricane-force winds that it generated. Within seconds, everything was transported to the underworld. The four horsemen of the apocalypse, Thanatos, the traitorous demons, and the mighty lord were brought back to the throne chamber.

His Majesty ascended to his throne and took his place. Its thorny branches instinctively beckoned to him. The god of the underworld watched the demons lying on the ground. They were all going to suffer eternally. With all of his strength, he laughed. He couldn't believe it himself. He was watched with concern by everyone present. The king stopped laughing without taking his eyes off the traitors. His face became the nightmare of thousands. "All you were naive, look how easily you were deceived by a divine messenger." He laughed out loud, unable to control himself.

"Stupid traitorous demons, from now on you all will crawl on the ground. You will never be able to stand up again. And will be condemned to suffer in the land of fire for eternity. You will be an example for others who think they can defeat the great Armaloth." Drickblood caught his attention now. Her shoulders shrugged as much as she could. Perhaps the king would feel pity for her. Yet, the king spared no one. Armaloth stretched out his arm and opened his hand. As if blown away like paper, Drickblood flew towards him. The king of the underworld grabbed her by the neck and put his face inches from hers.

"For you, Dickblood, I have a different destiny. You who dared to wear Persefore's crown, you who dared to get into my bed, and used me to hurt Moriah. I have a surprise for you. Armaloth raised his other arm, and black energy emitted from it. It was getting bigger and bigger. He threw it into the centre of the throne chamber once it no longer fit in the palm of his hand. As the ball of energy kept growing, it reached the ceiling. From it, you could hear sounds that terrified even the bravest. The four horsemen stood guard. The traitorous demons begged the god of darkness for mercy. And the former Queen, she could only scream and cry.

Within this ball of light was forming an imposing and frightening figure. A gigantic paw was first seen, then an animal's snout with fangs the size of a human arm. One of The Cerberus heads emerged from the black cloud, then another, then the other. The devil dog howled, causing the throne chamber to rumble.

Everyone was shocked at the vision in front of them. The Cerberus came out of the energy ball and looked at everyone who was present. But his eyes fiercely fixed on just one figure. And then, the hell dog took a few steps toward Drickblood. She, who was cornered and trembling in one of the corners. As if she could find pity in her dark lord, she begged not to take her away. Her pleas fell on deaf ears. The Cerberus opened his jaw. And between its hideous, pointed fangs, lifted the vampire from the ground. Not totally resigned to her fate, from the snout of the diabolical dog, she kept asking her king to forgive her.

The Cerberus turned and entered the energy ball again. Disappeared, taking Drickblood with him, forever.

Chapter 10

Time to purge my kingdom
Armaloth

One less problem to solve, now there are only eight left. All my attention was now focused on the remaining seven traitors. They were trapped in a corner. Cowards as they are, they only know how to attack from behind. Using my power, I reached out my hand and dragged the leader toward me.

Initially, I did not believe my spies when they told me Poissonaro was the primary instigator. Carldeath or Blooderek might have come to mind. Poissonaro, though? Among all the demons, he was the least likely.

As soon as he was in my presence, I dropped him to the floor and observed his disgusting form. His appearance is extremely repulsive, even for a demon. "Poissonaro, besides the clan leaders, who else is supporting this foolish insurgent movement? The demon before me trembled like a leaf in autumn. It was hard for him to speak coherently. I was only able to hear him babble, so I decided to help him out. As soon as I pointed my finger at one of his arms, his limb flew off. It was completely torn from his body. In pain, the nasty demon writhed on the ground. "Now, Poissonaro, I want to ask you again, who else was with you? He began to babble again, but this time his words seemed clearer.

By putting more pressure on his swollen neck, I lifted him closer to me and said, "I didn't hear you well, demon. SPEAK!" I lifted him by the neck and brought him closer to me. "Ma-ste-r" I dropped him to the ground, releasing his neck from my power. He raised his head with a lot of effort, and said, "The Dr-aug-n." Ah! Yes, I know, "Who else?" The demon was surprised to see that I already knew about the dragon's involvement. Seeing his countenance change, the demon looked down. And he said something that made my blood run cold, "He-ca-te"

I lost control of my energy and created a whirlwind that threw everyone into a downward spiral. Not even the four horsemen were able to withstand my power. I could not believe it. My mind felt like it had left my body. I heard something that was not possible. 'YOU'RE A LYING DEMON, SPEAK,' I shouted. My voice had become distorted, and it sounded like beast noises.

The demon did not last in front of this powerful energy, and began to unravel and then disintegrated in the air. The remaining seven also suffered the same fate. I was shocked when I saw what had happened. Then I closed my eyes and focused my energy into my centre, allowing the cyclical energy to cease. Falling backwards, I landed on my throne of thorns. The thorny branches immediately began to calm my being. Hecate, said the demon. And now he was no longer there to tell me more. While my gaze surveys the damage caused. Although the traitors were disintegrated. My Agalariept, Thanatos, and the four riders remained intact. I was watched by everyone, unable to comprehend what caused this display of power

"Hecate" was all I said. Thanatos and the four horsemen couldn't hide their shock upon hearing that name. "How?" Thanatos inquired. To which I replied, "I don't know, the demon mentioned her name." What to do now? Knowing that was the hardest part. Next, it was War's turn to speak. "Why would your mother want to destroy your kingdom? There's no doubt about it, she's been by your side all along." Yes, there must be more at stake. Unfortunately, the demons were no longer around to answer that question. "It might be nearly impossible to contact her. We demons are not welcome in the gods' land. Not even your Armaloth unless she is the one who looks for you first. I don't know how to do it. "She is a very complex and powerful goddess." Pestilence said

A solution suddenly popped into my head. I said, "The dragon demon." But then I remembered something very important. Moriah is with him. Then I got up from my throne and summoned my Agalariept. Upon my call, the infernal horse materialized in seconds. It was as if his eyes were blazing, he could feel the tension. And he also knew what I was thinking. Slowly, he approached me, resting his muzzle on my shoulder. As our energies synchronized, I was able to breathe easier. It seemed he knew something that I didn't, so I said, "Let's pay the Dragon Demon a visit." My dark steed nodded his head up and down. "Thanatos, find out more about the traitors in the clans. There must be more followers, and we have to finish them all. The god of death nodded his head and vanished into a black cloud.

"Riders, I need you with me. I know this dragon is more complicated than it appears. I don't understand his game, but I know one thing: he's extremely powerful. And very wise, his knowledge is equal to the number of centuries he has lived. I don't need to tell you that you must remain alert at all times." I rode my infernal steed and opened the seven beast dimension portal. The black incandescent ball parted in half. They followed me without wasting any more time. This time, the Dragon demon had a lot to explain.

After crossing the worlds, we finally reached the dimension of the dragon. At the moment of landing, the fire sphere disappeared. I looked around for the ancient beast, but he was nowhere in sight. Our path leads us to the mouth of the cave, where the dragon usually sleeps. However, it was empty. I was suddenly drawn to something. An intense smell of blood filled my nostrils, a smell that was familiar to me. It was from Moriah, I walked to where the strongest scent was. A dark spot covered that area of the ground. Touching it, I knew it was Moriah's dried blood. Suddenly, the traumatic memories of me torturing my wife ran through my head. As well as her pain, I could also sense her desperation to end her suffering. From what I could see, she lost a lot of blood. I closed my eyes and pulled my hand away.

Does this have anything to do with the dragon not being here? I need to know if Moriah is alive. I got up and walked back to my horse. Through the energy we shared, I began to feel his anguish. He needed his mistress, and I will see that she returns to us. Patting his head, I turned to see the riders. "I need the dragon." They looked at each other until

War stepped forward and extended his sword in front of him. The blade caught fire, and symbols appeared on it. The horseman saw them and raised his head and spied in all directions, then said, "The dragon is nearby." That's all he could say. Because a malevolent and powerful roar sounded from the heights.

An earthquake rumbled in the cave, the ground opened up, and the rocks began to crumble. A screech from the animal rattled the earth. We were being crushed by rocks and pieces of the roof. Therefore, I extended my hand to create an energy shield. Under it, we all remained safe until the shaking stopped. The worst was yet to come. An ancient, demonic force was surrounding us. It was beautiful. The lives of thousands of innocent people were poured into it. This beast was the soul eater. The Dragon demon had arrived. From the mouth of the cave, in the middle of the darkness, a pair of evil eyes flashed.

From his nose, he exhaled black smoke. Suddenly, the gigantic figure moved. He was heading in our direction. As if pulled by a powerful magnet, the weapons of the horsemen of the apocalypse fell to the ground. The dragon kept getting closer and closer. The Horsemen began to generate deadly energy, but nothing happened. It's as if they're empty. At last, the dragon's massive body emerged from the cave. The earth trembled under his footsteps. It was a terrifying sound. The horsemen of the apocalypse stood in front of the dragon, helpless. This beast possessed powerful ancient magic. Yet, my riders did not flinch, they stood straight ahead. Directly facing the beast. Pestilence leapt at him, but it was dragged back to the same spot. Their feet were tied to the ground. Other horsemen also attacked.

However, they were also grounded. The dragon looked at them with boredom, and that's when he turned his head and saw me straight in the eyes. "Child, are you back here again? And more so, you brought your friends to play, also!" The dragon turned his entire body in my direction and walked towards me. I was mere inches from his enormous figure. I had my Agalariept on guard. However, he did not seem concerned. Hi was giving the demon too much credit. As I raised my head and looked into his eyes, he returned the same intense look. There was an aura of hostility surrounding him now. Stronger than in our previous meeting. I must know what this dragon is thinking.

"Dragon Demon, surrender to me." But the beast only raised an eyebrow while exhaling smoke at the same time, laughing. "I am the king of demons. How dare you. The lord of the underworld." This seemed to silence him, his dark gaze returning: "You are only a weak demon, you are not worthy of the title you boast."

"True kings of demons wouldn't allow themselves to be manipulated." As he roared, the dragon shook the foundations of his own mountain. "ONLY A CREATURE SO WEAK CAN BE FOOLED SO EASILY."

"GRRRRR" The dragon blew a burst of fire at me. Despite forming my shield in time, the dragon's intensity was such that I was dominated by it. Flames penetrated my barrier, hitting my body and hurling me to the other side of the cave. My back hit the floor after that. Immediately, I stood up to defend myself. However, my dark steed got in the way. I was surprised, so I called him through the bond. He ignored me, yet, he continued to walk towards the dragon. Furthermore, he was watched carefully by the beast, but he did not attack.

I approached them very carefully, but my Agalariept stopped me. He stared at me intensely. Making sure I knew what he wanted. It was between him and the Dragon Demon. My horse shook his head once again as he faced the dragon. In contrast, the other one laughed and leaned back. My Agalariept shook its head from side to side. I had no idea what was going on. Until I hear the dragon say, "Okay, okay, you pesky creature. Can't I at least have a little fun with the boy for a bit? OK, OK." The dragon now turns his attention to me. I was still processing what I had seen.

After returning to its cave, the dragon fell to the ground. Only his head is visible. Suddenly, his eyes began to light up and the four horsemen of the apocalypse were released. They took their weapons from the floor, but they did nothing. The dragon followed their movements closely. "Why are you in my world, Armaloth, king of demons?" I was still recovering from the shock, when I said "Moriah, give her to me dragon demon." The dragon made an annoyed face and shook his head. "Moriah the human is not here, as you can see. King of the underworld, isn't it obvious? He raised an eyebrow as he said this. He exhaled smoke and replied, "Okay, I'll tell you where she is." He paused, and I could see in his eyes the seriousness of what he was about to say.

"King Armaloth, she has made a pact with me, and you will not be able to interfere." The dragon's gaze intensified with each passing second. But I was going to be left with my arms crossed. My anger was reaching its limits. I had to put this dragon in his place. I came for my wife, and I will return with her, pact or not. The deadly energy in my hands began to accumulate.

It began to spread throughout the place. My power was stealing life energy from all beings around me. I don't care about anyone at this point. The dragon had to pay for his insolence. But my Agalariept jumped in front of me, stopping me from unleashing more energy. Standing on two legs, he whinnied. He possessed the power of hell. Through his thorny branches, energy flowed. Hellfire engulfed his eyes. I was shocked more than I could have imagined.

When I lowered my arms, the energy I was generating disappeared. He delivered a clear message. I couldn't use my power against the dragon demon. My gaze briefly turned towards that infernal beast. But he seemed to be more annoyed than anything. My steed calmed down and returned to where he was, right next to the infernal beast. It didn't sit well with me. The dragon shook his head from side to side and said, "As I was telling you, boy, Moriah is not here. I sent her back to her world," I clenched my fists to contain the fury I was feeling and not attack him. "She asked me to do that, she is with her father, King Armaloth. But I need to warn you about something. You will not be able to approach her until our agreement is fulfilled."

"WHO DO YOU THINK YOU ARE DRAGON, TO TELL ME WHAT TO DO?" You are nothing anymore, a dead legend. This is my era, this is my time, and this is my reign." If I do not calm down, my power will spiral out of control. And through the bond that I share with my Agalariept, I felt his support. I closed my eyes and took a deep breath.

It is time to get this over with, and the dragon needs to tell me just what happened. My eyes opened to see things differently. And I adopted an attitude that provided me with the answers I sought. "Go on, dragon." He just exhaled smoke, his annoyance obvious.

"She returned to her world, as I mentioned. Moriah will be there, along with his father. Yet, you will not be able to intervene in her life. She will remain in her world until the term expires Naturally. Once that is done, she is all yours. King Armaloth, that was the deal. And I will make sure it is fulfilled. " Although my blood was boiling, I tried to remain calm as much as possible. There were still many things to know. "What is the deadline, dragon?" I asked. The dragon nodded and replied, "The last day of her father's life. The limit is that. Also, dark king, you owe me one. And this is the way that you're returning the favour. I'm not a charity, so there you have it, King."

"Moriah returns to the human world. In what way did this benefit you? You said you didn't do favours. Why would you help her escape?" Grinning wickedly, the dragon roared. "This is the thing, King Armaloth, nothing is free. In exchange for this small favour, she offers me her company." He must have seen my face, because he added Oh, Oh! No, you need not worry, king, I am not attracted to humans." The dragon's expression turned serious when he said, "I'm not saying it will be every day. More likely, one or two times per week. Like a friend's reunion or something like that. "I promise you, king of the underworld, that I will never put the queen in danger or touch a single one of her hair. I live that to you." I turned to see my Agalariept, and he nodded his head, shaking it up and down several times. Three against one, what else can I do?

Moriah, enjoy your time on earth because the time will come. It will be impossible for you to escape. But they didn't say anything about her not being watched. Nodding my head, I accepted the situation. "Dragon, I will honour this pact and consider this debt paid. But there is still something that I want to know. I want you to clarify something for me. How is Hecate related to you and the traitors?" The dragon raised his head suddenly, hitting the ceiling of his cave. When he recovered from the impact, he looked side to side and sighed. "Hecate, she was the one who alerted me to what was going on. She possesses a magical power that is unrivalled. During the night, she hears the greatest secrets. We discussed this. It's thanks to her, your mother. You're still here, boy. And Moriah will have time to recover from what you did to her."

"But Hecate and I will help her adjust to her new world. It is our opinion that the underworld needs powerful rulers. Thus, king Armaloth, your mother and I will educate Moriah in the dark arts." Upon hearing this, my stomach clenched. There is no possibility of my mother betraying me. I had always had her on my side. Innumerable times, she has done so. Having said that, there was nothing left for me to do. I opened the portal to my world and brought everyone with me. To hell.

Chapter 11

After all
Moriah

Since I returned, my perception of life has changed dramatically. Life is very short, I know that. And there are so many things to figure out, and so much to do, that there is not enough time. Despite my longing for love, I will not be able to enjoy it as I want. I have been robbed of that opportunity. Neither will I be able to carry my own children in my arms. Human babies, the way they should be.

Those are the only things that make me sad. Family members strolling nonchalantly down in the park without a care in the world. Since the devil might not come for them one day. There are times when that is all I can think about, the fear that one day that will come. However, I still have my father. The reason I fought so hard to be back in my world is because of him. Despite the fact that I am safe for the time being, I cannot relax my mind. I live in constant fear of what might happen. Or what happens there. I was traumatized in a very serious way. The scars on my body are all healed, but unfortunately, they still remain. That's the only thing that couldn't be healed. Every time I look at it, I am reminded of what I experienced.

I must wear clothes that completely cover my body. It doesn't matter how hot it is, nor can I enjoy the beautiful beaches of France. My back is almost entirely covered in scars, whether they are from the knife, the whip, or the fangs. Likewise, my legs also suffer from this problem. As for my neck, I have to cover it with scarves. Because this is where the marks of the fangs and punctures of the claws are more evident.

I will have to hide my body for the moment, but not forever. Having plastic surgery is a thought I have considered, at least where my skin is most exposed. As for the rest of my body, it is a lot to accomplish all at once. Five months have passed since I came out of hell. I would avoid going back if I could. It is not possible for me to find a way, and I don't believe there is one. In this time, only reflection has taken place. I have come to the conclusion that the rest of my life on earth will be spent fully.

I won't waste my time worrying about being the best or about trivialities. No, this time everything is different. I will not let this opportunity pass me by. The lesson I learned was very valuable. And that is, not wasting my life. As I pondered all this, I decided, timidly and reluctantly, to tell my dad what had happened. It's impossible to tell if he'd believe me or not. But when he hugged me with all his strength after hearing what I said, my eyes filled with tears. Even though I didn't tell him all, what he heard was enough to get an idea of what I went through.

But what surprised me the most was when he confessed to me what he did. "Moriah, daughter, there are things that, as I told you, are difficult to explain, much less to prove. Even so, I prayed to any god, or angel who would listen to me, for your well-being. As I knew something was wrong with you. However, there was no way to show you. Seeing it with your own eyes would have given you a far greater understanding of it." And so it was, my dad prayed for my health. That's right, the biggest contradiction in the world, a praying psychiatrist, ha, ha, ha. My father is one of a kind.

I will now dedicate my whole life to him. I will regain all the time we lost due to our ignorance. But for now, I need to make a phone call. "Hi, Carla, this is Moriah. How is the moving going? OKAY. Okay, email me the reference number. My new place is not ready yet, so I need to finish it before everything arrives. Keep me posted, OK, thanks, bye."

"Dad, Carla already sent my office stuff today. She agrees to send me the reference number by email. We must hurry to finish the new clinic. The glass of water my dad was drinking was placed on the table, as he wiped his mouth with a napkin.

"Oh, that was faster than I had thought. Your assistant is well-trained." He looked at me with concern in his eyes. "I don't think we are ready to receive everything, daughter. There is still much to be done. My dad was worrying more than necessary. I told him, "Don't worry, everything will be fine. We can hire staff to finish everything. If it's money, don't worry." While smiling, I raised and lowered my eyebrows with mischievous expressions. "I have a lot of money, dad, and I'm going to get more.

Ha, ha, ha. As a matter of fact, I have no idea what we

will do with all the money that will be raining down on us very soon. It was a successful deal. That we closed with the pharmaceutical company to have our formula marketed. Despite my knowledge of its excellent quality, I was not expecting this kind of success." I laughed out loud, it's so good when things work out for us. My dad saw me with a keep your feet on the wrong face, and joined my happiness. We both fell into a pleasant silence after that. Until my cell phone rang. I took it from the table and replied "Hello."

"Good afternoon, are you Miss. Moriah Regina?" A stranger asked, "Yes, that's right, it's me. What can I do for you?" The stranger paused for a moment and then said. "It is an honour to meet you. I am the executive of the real estate agency. You asked us to find you a place to function as a medical facility. And with pleasure I want to inform you that we have already found the proper place.

And it has all the specifications that you asked for. When can you come and see it?" I looked at my dad immediately, and my smile got bigger; he looked at me suspiciously, and I replied, "Right now." After he gave me the address, my dad and I left. It's the moment we've been waiting for, everything will have to go smoothly. There is no doubt in my mind about that.

The place was half an hour's drive from my dad's house, now mine too. After I told him of my plans to move in with him, his face changed. It looked like it had been lit up. My heart was so filled with love when he smiled at me, I couldn't stop thinking about how much I love him. I couldn't help but hug him, as I'd always wanted to.

From now on, he will have to get used to my hugs. Arriving at the place, we got out of the car and went to the building. From a distance, it looked like a perfect three-story building. The executive was standing in the entrance waiting for us. He greeted us and asked us to follow him. The first thing I noticed was the high level of security. The waiting room was exactly how I imagined it to be, and the reception was very spacious.

My new clinic will be perfect in this location. I discussed this with my dad, and he was willing to help me in any way he could. In some cases, he was willing to work with me. Already, that's progress. As we continued to tour the building, we noticed that each level had several rooms. Those could be used as offices, meeting rooms, inspection rooms.

There was an immense amount of opportunity. We left the building after finishing the tour, and my dad and I looked at each other briefly, then I said to the Executive, "I'll take it." This is how I became the first specialized psychiatry clinic in the region. We just had to adjust the place to our needs, and wait for the move to arrive from London. Carla and five more of my assistants liked the idea of working here with me and moving out of London.

****

Over the course of the week, everything from my penthouse and my London office had already been moved. My new clinic was finally finished already. We had one more week during which everything was detailed, so that a date was finally set for our opening. The day we opened was a great success. I remember that very well. Members of psychiatric associations as well as colleagues were invited. Not only from France, but from the US, London, Italy, and Germany as well. The facilities were first-rate, and the equipment we acquired was high-tech.

As time passed, we began to receive patients. Every doctor we hired provided their patients with respectful care and treated them responsibly. That's what my dad taught me. I had successfully re-established myself in the human world. Now the only thing I wanted to do was erase the scars from my body. I got tired of hiding all the time. And on my face, I had to wear a lot of makeup, to hide some. I wanted to get rid of them for good.

As a result, I saw a plastic surgeon. I was asked to show the doctor which scars I wanted to erase. When I did, he stayed still. His face said it all, as I watched him the entire time. He felt sorry for my situation. The only thing I told him was that I had been tortured. He understood perfectly and told me that we would start with the most visible places.

And so we did. In a month I had already freed myself from the scars on my face, neck and arms. There were small signs left, but the doctor told me that there was no point in operating again. The remnants weren't worth it, since the lines were barely visible. I agreed. At least I wouldn't see them anymore. I would need longer to cleanse my entire body.

****

It had been two years since I had returned. I was already

feeling better mentally and spiritually. It is not easy to recover from the terrible experiences I have endured. Nevertheless, thanks to my father and my work, I was able to succeed.

Today is a good example. The pharmaceutical company that bought our patent will launch the new medicine on the market today. They named it Codin-regina. As a tribute to its creators. My dad and I were the guests of honour at this magnificent event. Which will mark history in the field of medicine. My dad was so stylish. He chose a black suit, English cut. Funny, since the event is in a branch in Germany. So here we are enjoying the original frankfurters. I decided a long sleeveless navy blue dress with a low neckline. I no longer have to hide from anything.

My skin looks like any other person's. My mind immediately went to the dragon. I can see that he is keeping his word, and he will give me all the time we agreed to. I only wish that day did not come, or at least, that day was very far away.

After the event, my dad and I decided to tour Germany. We both worked hard, so a little break would be very beneficial. Like everywhere else in Europe, the people here are cold. However, the country is wonderful, its architecture and culture are amazing. And what about beer and food? Our trip lasted for a week, unfortunately we weren't able to stay longer. We had a lot of responsibilities on our shoulders. The clinic was a great success, both in the treatment of patients and its fame. Our team was the best. Carla, I no longer had her as my assistant; now she was my administrator. Basically, she runs the clinic. That's how amazing she is. I knew she had so much potential, but now I'm seeing it.

One day, she came to me with news that made me very happy, but at the same time saddened me. She was pregnant with her first baby. She and her husband Pier were so happy. They met a few months after arriving from London. They got married a year ago. And this is the result. Love is evident in their relationship, and I am envious of it. However, I wished her all the happiness in the world.

For my part, I know that I will not have it. That's why I don't get romantically involved with anyone. I know it's dangerous, and I don't know what would happen if I did. I better not risk it. So here I am, an unmarried woman alone in the world. Time kept passing, and the people around me came and went. I had only two constants in my life: my dad and the clinic. Then one day, I noticed something that shocked me. In fact, I had a mental breakdown when I realized what was going on.

The other day I was complimented by a patient on how young I looked. She wants me to give her the details of my plastic surgeon. Thanking her, I took it as a compliment. But for the next week, that comment was always in the back of my brain. Always present, until I discovered something that horrified me. My dad was getting older, people were changing. My employees' children had grown up. And my friends gain extra weight.

Or their hair was painted white. Their lines around the eyes were more visible. In addition, they are complaining now that they are no longer young. I was in my room getting ready for sleep and thinking about this, when the realization of all this hit me. There was no change in me, I wasn't ageing. I ran to the bathroom, stood in front of the mirror and looked at myself carefully. It was true, I was still the same. Nothing in me had changed.

The skin on my face was firm and without wrinkles. The tone of my muscles was in good condition. There was no pain or illness in my body. As far as I can remember, I haven't become ill since I got back. I was completely shocked by this discovery. What does this mean? Could it be that I would never get old? Now what? My dad might be able to tell me something. Whatever it is. After leaving my room, I ran down the stairs. My dad was sitting on the couch reading a magazine while drinking tea.

As I walked over to where he was, I stood in front of him without saying a word. The thought of him saying anything about all this made me very nervous. Once he saw me, a suspicious look crossed his face. "Dad, can you tell me something?" I asked as He looked at me without saying anything. "Physically, have I changed anything since I returned from that place?" I asked. Anguish was eating me up. I felt like my stomach was in knots. I watched in astonishment as my father's eyes widened. As he gripped my arms tightly, he looked at me very closely and said, "Moriah, daughter, the words don't come to me. I see you the same way as always. It is possible, however, that what you suggest is true."

"Not counting plastic surgery to fix your skin. No other surgical procedures have been performed on you. However, it is still too early to make a judgment. There will be many theories we can put together, but we won't really know what it is. Our best bet is to observe you better, time will tell." He hugged me and I put my head on his shoulder, and then he said, "Don't worry, love, you'll get over this too.

My daughter is extremely intelligent and always finds a way to overcome obstacles." He wiped the tears that had escaped my eyes with his finger as we finished the hug. "For dinner, how about that chilli con carne we bought at the Mexican food store the other day? It looks wonderful, come on." I smiled at him from the bottom of my heart. He did it again. I linked my arms with his, and we walked into the kitchen.

Chapter 12

Time passed by
Moriah

Standing in front of a sideboard in a cosmetics store. According to the Internet, productions for theatre or television use this brand. There was information that said it was very good to give a change of appearance to the face.

Additionally, I can see accessories to complete the look. Scars and silicone masks, for instance. Wigs, extensions, fake fillers, and costumes are available. There are a lot of things. This might be the place I've been looking for. My dad looked at me and nodded that this was the right place. Then we went inside. When I entered this place, I felt like I was in another world. It is amazing how human beings can create these types of items. They are generally used for entertainment, but not in my case. I want to change my appearance.

Then, I saw a wide-eyed look on my dad's face. His first encounter with alien costumes must have been strong enough to evoke such a reaction. Wow! It seems so real. Taking a chance to touch it, he reached out. Then, he just shook his head. After that, we kept looking for the perfect costume for me, strolling around the store. Finally, we arrive at the section on wigs and extensions. I had to choose one that was as close as possible to my original hair. But with a touch of grey. My purpose in being here is to make myself look older. Almost sixteen years have passed since that day. As for my body, it still looks exactly like when I was 27 years old. My body should now resemble that of a 43-year-old woman. I need all of this because of that. People will become suspicious. And the excuses of plastic surgery are no longer credible.

Compared to my dad, who has already begun to reflect on his years. His 73rd birthday was a month ago. Although he has a strong body, his vitality has decreased considerably. Now, he requires more attention and a special diet. And because he is the only one I have, I need to pay more attention to him.

But going back to the wigs, I found some discreet extensions, which matched my natural hair colour. With some grey hair, I can put those under my hair without showing them. This will also give the impression that my hair is old. I bought it as my first purchase because it's perfect. I then continued with the makeup, even buying the silicone wrinkles. The saleswoman explained the process of applying them to me. Additionally, she told me that I need to practice a lot to make them look natural. As a result, she suggested taking makeup courses. My answer was, of course, yes. I want to appear as natural as possible.

We left the store happy that we had found what we were looking for. Afterwards, I treated my dad to French food at a nearby restaurant. He loves French cuisine. I am however very concerned about something. Dad's health is rapidly deteriorating. His eyes show how exhausted he is. Currently, he continues to work with me. But I am seriously thinking of reducing his hours, and days. I've even thought about hiring a nurse to help him with everything. While I am working.

It is too early to tell, so I will schedule three full physical exams a year to keep tabs on his health. We can then determine if something is wrong and treat it before it becomes worse. His health is the most important thing to me. While it's in my hands, I will not skimp on anything so that he is well. Having finished our meal, we returned to the house. We had bought enough bags to look like a Christmas tree. As well, we stop to shop for clothes. The section forty and higher was where I went.

The styles are so different from what I am used to, but everything has to match. When we arrive at the house. I walked to my room to leave my purchases. Then go downstairs and make some sandwiches. My dad really enjoys tea in the afternoons. So here I am, preparing an afternoon tea.

Once everything had been prepared, I found him lying on the couch. With the television on, asleep. Evidently, he was tired. So I grab a blanket and cover him up. Then I let my dad rest for the rest of the day. In the meantime, I was able to hack the appointment with the hospital and hire the best nurse in France.

****

As time passed, it had already been 26 years since the incident. My life has been peaceful, and I have achieved everything that I have set as a goal. It has been a successful life for me. But sometimes, I feel empty. There have been many years living as a single woman. I have my dad with me, but it isn't the same as having my own family. It is the only thorn in my side. I have begun organizing all my things. I have thought about this for the past few years. What will happen to all that I have accomplished on that day? Consequently, I decided to negotiate the transfer of my clinic and my business.

I choose an association that will be in charge of administering and maintaining my legacy. Unfortunately, I don't have anyone to pass it on to. As my father grows older, I am heartbroken to see him suffer. His body can be relieved of pain with medicine. Nevertheless, they keep returning. Seeing how dependent the body is on medication is very painful. But at least he won't have to suffer.

Every night when I put him to bed, he tells me about my childhood. Of what a smart kid that I always was. His belief was that I would accomplish great things in my life. It's impossible to not shed a few tears when I listen to him speak. I stayed with him until he fell asleep, listening. It was a tough time. My feeling of being alone grew. I could feel in my bones that he didn't have much time left. Then I tortured myself, thinking that his life was being shortened considerably. He rarely went out anymore; his life was confined to these four walls. His weakened body wasn't allowing him to leave. I know it was inevitable, and that it had to be very strong. I couldn't crack in front of him. For both of us, I had to be strong. Because of this, I only allowed myself to cry in my room, behind closed doors. Only there, I could take out all the pain I had when

I saw his life slip from his hands.

He is the only person who knows my secrets. I did not tell him about the part where the king would come back for me. That will be the last day of his life. How can I tell him that? It would be best if he never knew that my future was still in the devil's hands.

The following days passed in the same way. Wearing the costume became second nature to me. Everyone could be fooled by the results. What I learned from this course has served me well. This result would not have been possible without them. And as time passes, I just have to increase more grey hair or more wrinkles. I've considered putting on some padding. Since my body is thin as always. This body would not fool anyone. But how annoying it would be to have to carry around extra things. It's better to buy baggy clothes instead.

****

Several more years passed. My businesses were already controlled by the association with which I made the agreement. Most of my time was spent with my father at home. His condition was deteriorating. He spent more time sleeping than awake. It was my duty to be with him. In the same way that he was always with me.

To see him in such a state pains me so much. My father, my rock. The only person I had in this life. He was leaving me. However, I knew it was inevitable. We did not know how long he was going to live. But whatever it was, I would spend it by his side. I couldn't let a minute waste away from him. I was going to make the most of every moment we had together. So I moved to his room, I was his head nurse. A doctor checked on him personally every week. This is how we spend our time.

I stopped going out, I could only be next to my dad. As far as my job responsibilities were concerned, I discussed them over the phone. Or by online conference. However, in the end, I had to let go of everything. Knowing what might happen to me has made me more cautious. I could be taken from this life at any moment. The responsibilities I had weren't going to be left hanging in the air

Therefore, I give it all up. I was no longer a psychiatrist, nor a consultant, or a businesswoman. I relegated myself to the role of a daughter. She was only concerned about her dad's health. That was my sole responsibility. And that's how I wanted it. I had to be in his last moments of life, with him. I didn't know what the future held for me, but no one could rob me of taking with me the last memories of my life with my dad. So, day and night I pass by his side. Day and night I was awake, on the lookout for what he needed. I was the nurse who was most dedicated to her patient. The best daughter has set foot on this earth. I was only looking for the moment when he awoke. Just to be able to look into those beautiful eyes once more. No matter how old he got, his eyes stayed the same, beautiful and full of love towards me. They were so clear, that sometimes I could see what he was thinking through them. I knew the moment would come, but I hoped it would take much, much longer.

The days passed as usual. Never did I leave his side. I did not bathe for fear of returning and not finding him with me. The monitor we installed next to his bed was constantly telling me how his heart was behaving. Next to us was a resuscitator. In case we need it. We had already used it twice, when his heart stopped for a few seconds. It was a nightmare during those minutes. Fortunately, I always have a team of medical professionals nearby. They are more than capable of doing their work with excellence.

They have saved his life more than once. Whenever he was awake, he did not tell me stories from my childhood any more. He could no longer speak. So it was my turn to tell him about the clinic and all the lives we had improved through our work. My dad smiled weakly at me, so I knew he was still with me. He still understood me. Seeing my dad's life end was heartbreaking to me. It wasn't long before it was over. The doctors didn't give him more.

Whenever I said goodbye to him, I would kiss his forehead. Every night, I would take his hand and kiss it. Every night, I stroked his hair. I didn't know if this would be the last day that I could touch him, or kiss him. I did not know, I did not know it. And that's how the next morning I found his body cold. During his sleep, my dad passed away peacefully. At that moment, I knew what true loneliness was. My father, my only friend, my partner, my mentor. He was gone forever. Rest in peace, Philip Regina. Brilliant Psychiatrist and exceptional father.

****

Years ago, arrangements were made for his funeral. Upon leaving, everything had been prepared. I had everything ready. The funerary took my dad's body to prepare it. He will be buried like a king. I had a calm expression on my face. But inside, I was shattered. Nothing, not even the threat of being taken from this world, could keep my mind from my father. Then, I couldn't get out of the deep pain I felt for the loss of my dad. I was walking because I had legs, and I was talking because I had a mouth. But my mind was not here. It left with my dad. But I was not surprised when I saw hundreds of people at his funeral who had come to say goodbye to him.

This only reaffirmed the quality of a man that he was. I was so proud of him. People approached me and offered their condolences and their full support. I could only thank them for showing a calm demeanour. The only reason I wasn't lying on the floor crying in despair, was because in my mind, I was only listening to his words. *"Don't worry, love, you will get over this too. My daughter is very intelligent and always knows how to overcome any obstacle."* As I remember this, I shed the first tears since leaving his body at the funerary. I couldn't stop myself, for several minutes my pain flowed in the form of tears. But, eventually, I managed to calm down to attend to those who came to say goodbye to my dad.

After the farewell ceremony ended. It was time to take him to the place where his remains will rest forever.

In the back seat of the car, I spent about half an hour on the road. As I turned my head back, I noticed a long line of cars following us to the cemetery. I was not surprised by this; it filled me with pride. The qualities my dad possessed were incomparable. Turning my head forward, I fixed my gaze on the road. Arriving at the cemetery. The coffin was taken to the mausoleum, where everything was ready for burial. All of us follow him in silence.

There was a sense of loss in the air when a great person passed away. The crowd gathered around my father's remains. A few minutes later, the priest began to give his sermon and say the final goodbye. At that point, I could not hear anything going on around me. The whole experience felt surreal. As if my mind were silently watching everything from above. It was as if I had left my body. I also wanted to go with him, so that he wouldn't leave me.

Then, I felt his hand touch my shoulder for a moment. He always did this when he saw me worried or upset. As if his spirit was around me, I could feel it. Keeping my composure, I wiped away the tears that I couldn't hold back. Until now, and even now, he is still with me, supporting me, giving me strength. At that moment, I lifted my head and looked up at the sky. The wind was blowing on my face. That's when my body shuddered. A tangle of invisible arms seemed to encircle around me. Then, the wind whispered into my ear, *"I love you, Moriah."* I fell to the ground on my knees, crying, and hugging myself. I cried like I'd never imagined possible. Oh! How much alone I was.

People were around me, but nothing mattered to me. Then someone picked me up by the arm and I got up off the ground. The minutes passed and people began to leave. One by one, they said their goodbyes until none remained. With my body empty, I remain in the same place. In front of my dad's grave, I was left alone. My skin was gently caressed by the wind, and my hair fluttered. Afterwards, I felt an immense peace.

I knew my father was fine, wherever he was, and he

would always look out for me. He always has, and death will not stop him from doing so. "See you soon, my father, rest in peace." After that, I contemplated his grave one more time. However, in the next moment, everything around me became ice. Standing there, I couldn't think or move. I felt electricity shivering down my spine, and the hairs on my skin rose.

"The time has come for you to go home, Moriah. Come with me, come to your husband"

Chapter 13

Back in his arms
Moriah

I can't move, I feel like my feet are anchored to the floor. My muscles are not responding to me. My brain, as well as my surroundings, is frozen. I knew this could happen at any time. But, I thought I was strong enough to accept my fate. Now I see that it's not the case. I'm cowering, and I can feel the panic start to take over my mind. I also know that I can't do anything. But I'm not ready to go back to that place. So I tried to move my body, I had to face him. I will tell him what I think. So I turned my body in his direction so slowly, I thought I would never make it. And the image that greeted me when I saw him made my stomach turn. I had already forgotten how terrifying and repulsive this being is.

Armaloth was standing in front of me, his evil presence surrounding us. With his intense eyes, he was watching me closely. Why? I wondered over and over, why couldn't I live and die like everyone else? What was different about me that made them set their eyes on me?

I thought I could tell him something, but the words just

weren't forming. Nothing came out of my mouth. What little courage I thought I had, it evaporated. My legs started shaking. My tears started to come out, it was too much. I was lost and doomed, and nobody, or anything, was going to be able to help me. Suddenly, the king raised his arm and offered me his hand. We were a good distance apart, separated from each other.

I had to go to him, as always. But how to make my legs move? Probably, the same fear of not obeying him made me do it. One-step and then the other, my tears kept spilt. My end was near, I knew what would await me in his world. But in the next moment, my father's loving words reached me. Like thunder crashing through the land. *"My daughter is very intelligent"*

And at that moment I understood that if I wanted to survive in that world. I would have to make it mine too. I understood everything at that moment. Like the revelation that had been hidden from my eyes. I would have to fight ferociously, but most of all with intelligence. Against all of them, that wanted to hurt me. And I also knew that now, I had allies. No more was I alone, in fact, I never was.

The dark horse and the tree of knowledge were always on my side. I just never saw it that way. And now, I have the mighty dragon demon watching my back. A strange heat began to consume my heart. And a single thought was the one that spun in my mind. *"Take your place, Moriah. The true wife of the king of the underworld. Embrace the crown and own it"*

Now, my steps were steady. I walked towards my destiny,

with the strength that I never thought I had. The king's hand was within reach, and without hesitation, I took it. There was an exchange of energy, which stunned me for a few seconds, making me close my eyes. Later, when I opened them, my eyes were no longer the same. Armaloth no longer looked repulsive or nauseating. Now, he was powerful. He was the most amazing creature I had ever seen. His greyish skin now shone like the reflection of a crystal.

I couldn't stop staring at him in amazement. I was captivated by his very presence. This being in front of me was my husband. My destiny and I was tired of denying it. That was my mistake from the beginning. Not having embraced their evil. So, I looked him in the eye, and without letting go of his hand, I said "Armaloth, husband, I'm ready." My husband smiled and nodded his head in approval. He pulled my arm closer to his body.

And that's when I was able to soak up his essence. I couldn't help but get closer, and breathe him in. I laid my head on his shoulder and let his power comfort me. Not only that, but I closed my eyes and the only thing I felt after, was a tremor around us. The next time I opened them, I was no longer in my world.

****

When I opened my eyes, I was surprised to see that we were in the throne chamber. What I notice immediately, are the thorny branches snaking in my direction. The next thing I knew, I was hugged by them. The thorny branches tangled all over my body. Its thorns dug painfully into my skin. I was already unaccustomed to its enthusiasm, and how much it hurt. But after a while, the pain disappeared. The only thing I could do is return the hug by caressing them. I don't know how, but I had missed them. They were always with me, protecting me. Afterwards, I felt another presence in the chamber, long before I saw who it was. He was calling me, demanding my attention.

I turned my head in the direction of where this presence had manifested. And that's when I saw him emerge from a powerful, dark cloud of energy. My saviour, my fire horse. He trotted gently towards me, wagging his tail sideways. Already being a few inches away from me, he stopped, and I raised my hand and stroked his snout. He closed his eyes and rested his head on my shoulder. I could feel his energy welcoming me. Also, feel the happiness that my presence brought him.

Together, the thorny branches, the fire horse and I, we remained entwined for a long time. The energy we were sharing was so warm and peaceful. And at the same time, I was healing the pain that was still in my heart. I could feel it running through every one of my cells. And after a while of being hugged, I remembered something very important. I released my horse, which still did not know his name. And I turned my head to where Armaloth was watching us interact. His gaze was full of intensity, and something I could not decipher what it was.

"Where is she?" Armaloth was surprised by my question, if only for an instant. But he immediately regained his old face. He nodded his head and just said "Fine, I'll show you" Afterwards, he waved his arm in the air, an image appeared out of nowhere. So, I put my full attention on the pictures that were forming. And when I saw what it was, a sigh left my lips. A gigantic three-headed dog was in front of a body lying on the ground.

I focused my vision to identify that demon on the floor, and I could recognize who she was. It was her. Queen Drickblood, my torment. She, along with Armaloth and his demons, made me hate my existence. To the degree of preferring death a thousand times, before continuing to endure this life. Her strong, muscular and indestructible body. The same one with which she used to terrify and wound me, now it was undone. Without strength, torn to pieces. Her skin was hanging from the bones. She was nothing now. For the first time in my life, I was glad that someone was suffering like she was.

Then I turned my attention to Armaloth. And with my glare filled with resentment, I said, "Why aren't you there with her, sharing the same punishment? Don't think I have forgotten what you did to me." The king's eyes turned dark as an abyss. And with the wave of his hand, my body flew to where he was. For a moment, panic seized my stomach. All the memories of what he did to me came back like a tsunami, washing away everything in its path. But my father's words were constantly ringing in my head and were stronger than my fear.

I have to be able to stand on my two feet. It's up to me now, what kind of life I'll have here is I don't?

My body slammed against his chest. And I felt myself crash against a concrete wall. Air escaped from my lungs on impact. After a few seconds trying to inhale oxygen, Armaloth took a fist of my hair and pulled my head back painfully. This made me face him, and my eyes collided with his. Everything was repeating it again, and he would never stop abusing me. The fear that had taken hold of me before began to wane as my father's words were repeated over and over again.

"My daughter is very smart, my daughter is very smart, my daughter is very smart." Over and over again, this filled me with courage, and what he told me convinced me that it was true. I was very intelligent and for someone who had reached the top, never again, this demon was going to abuse me, never. So looking into his eyes. And without hesitation, I said, "Armaloth. If you think you have the right to abuse me because you are the king of this world, you are wrong. What you and she did to me, that, never I'll forget it. And let me tell you one thing. The first time I got here, I was alone, but now I'm not. "

I nodded at the horse and the thorny branches. Armaloth turned to see them briefly and then returned his gaze to me again. His face showed how unhappy he was. "I can make your life miserable, think about it. Besides, if you don't behave as you should with me, and you don't keep me happy, I already have a place to go. My new friend also has a very bad temper. And he breathes fire from his mouth," Armaloth's eyes were wide open, in a comical way. Without taking my eyes off him, I freed myself from his grip and said, "So, you know now. From now on, you will respect me, and at the first display of aggressiveness towards me. I will go to live with the Dragon." My husband gritted his teeth, he was so angry. But the fire horse and the thorny branches approached me, flanking me. My husband watched this in amazement, and then it surprised me because he started to laugh out loud. I didn't know what to expect from this. I was biting my tongue on nerves. So I just waited for him to finish.

Finally, after what seemed like hours, my husband finished laughing. And without warning, he kissed me. My brain couldn't react to what was happening. This really left me speechless. He kissed me like he was hungry, like he missed me, like he couldn't get enough of me. His kiss was so erotic, that I started kissing him the same way. He pulled away abruptly and pressed his forehead to mine. Then he told me, "My queen, never again I will allow you to leave my side. And not even that nosy dragon will keep me away from you." He held my hair tighter and looked into my eyes. And I could see thousands of emotions unfold through them.

"My queen, do you understand?" I nodded my head as a sign that I understood very well what he was saying. He would respect me enough not to give me an excuse for wanting to leave. At that moment, I knew that my life here would not be as bad as I first imagined. And if Armaloth was willing to keep me happy, I would do the same. Anyway, I said, "I still hope to see a punishment for what you did to me." My husband hugged me tight, pinching my waist. "I am King Moriah, do not push your luck." With that said, he took my lips with his, telling me everything I wanted to know.

****

The kiss turned into a real battle. In spite of everything, I felt hunger and desire for him. Armaloth lifted me up, and I laced my legs around his waist. Our lips did not part. His hands were everywhere. My body was eager to receive its Lord. It had been so long since I last did it. I hesitated a bit, but the desire won the battle. His pointed teeth scraped my skin, but it didn't hurt as it used to, in fact, it turned me on more.

And knowing that those fangs could pierce my skin at any moment filled my stomach with explosions. Being in his arms, I now knew how much I had missed him. He once told me something that I didn't want to believe. And it was that my body would recognize its master. Now I know, and it's true. The clothes I was wearing ended up torn all over the place. Now his tongue was all over my body. He caught my nipple with his fangs, and bit down hard. That drove me high. Then, I felt my blood run down my side. His wonder-working tongue was licking every drop.

Armaloth took my face with both of his hands. His fangs and lips were red with my blood. He reached over and kissed me, making me taste my own essence. I couldn't understand what it felt like to try it. Then, my eyes widened, and my tongue wanted more. I kissed him as if I had been deprived of water. I bite his tongue until I taste his. My husband growled into my mouth, but I never let go of him. His tongue was caught between my teeth. I began to devour it as if it were my last meal on this earth. And then I felt his claws scratching my inner thigh. I couldn't take it anymore, and I raised my pelvis, offering myself to him. My King understood what I wanted. And with desperation matching mine, he took his penis and aligned it at my entrance. He rammed me with the force that he could only give me. I felt it hit my insides. My flesh was being slaughtered with his thorns, but I did not cower. His manhood was endless.

My hips moved to his rhythm, pounding in the places it counted. My orgasm was catching up with me until I couldn't hold it back anymore. Pleasure erupt like incandescent lava, bathing my entire being. My walls continued to convulse with pleasure. Squeezing it, until I heard a howl that penetrated the thick layer of darkness that surrounded us.

My husband exploded inside me, caressing my womb with his essence. It drove me crazy again. I was elated, asking for more, more, "Give me more, I want more Oh! Another orgasm appeared out of nowhere. He kept pouring his sperm on me, it seemed endless. And the important thing is that I did not want it to end. I ended up exhausted and without strength. My body felt like jelly. Armaloth was still on top of me. His burly body traps me more than it already was. He got up, leaning on his elbows, and looked down at me. I'm sure my face was a sight to behold.

Then, without taking his eyes off me, he said "You are mine, Moriah, My queen. The entire demonic world will know who you are, and to whom you belong. But before that, you have to receive the crown of Persephone. There is no turning back for you. Your new life begins now. By my side." I blinked several times, absorbing it all. Afterwards, I gave him a tired smile. I already knew that I had no other way out, that I had no other options. But right now, I wanted nothing more than to be in his arms." Armaloth brought his face to my neck and inhaled sharply. Then he lay on top of me, and that's when I felt like the earth was swallowing us. I closed my eyes, trusting him.

Chapter 14

The Tattoo
Armaloth

I opened my eyes even with fatigue, the whole night we spent enjoying each other. Trying to make up for the time we lost. There was a moment when I thought I would never stop. Moriah had awakened in me that all-consuming hunger.

And it is something that only she could quench. I lowered my gaze and saw my wife, who was sleeping peacefully in my arms.

It has been so long since I felt her body next to mine. I longed for the moment her skin touched mine. Have her by my side, in my bed. My wife had finally returned home. And I couldn't be more alert to her presence. I could smell her, feel her. Just by closing my eyes, I knew what she was doing. She has consumed all my thoughts. This time apart from her, I learned something that I could never have known. It is that I needed something desperately from her. As I watched her interact with those in her world, I saw how important she was. How high she had risen, and how independently she had achieved it. Observe how she makes her decisions and how intelligently she does things.

Seeing her from afar, I felt consumed with desire. As I stood by, I grew darker and darker as I thought about her. I was blinded by my desire to consume it all. My only thought was to destroy and corrupt. Fortunately, I had my Agalariept and my thorny branches with me. Giving me the energy I need to curb that insatiable thirst. Many times, I was on the verge of breaking the pact with the dragon. The consequences were nothing to me, I just wanted to have her back. I felt that my need for her was growing more and more each day. And it was something that I was having a hard time controlling.

I, the omnipotent King Armaloth, caught in the clutches of a human. This I denied for a long time, but in the end, that only reaffirms what I already knew. I was his. And even though I knew that she would one day return to me, that was no longer enough for me. I wanted to have the devotion and love that she gave to the human who fathered her. Even though I was jealous, something important happened during her absence. Patience, I knew that the day would come when she would submit to me. And not because I forced her, but because she had chosen to do so. And despite what I did to her, she didn't take a single step back. Other than that, she surprised me with her courage and strength.

The ultimatum she gave me really surprised me. I laughed out loud. It was so refreshing to have someone dare to challenge me like that. She did it with such grace that I could have given her anything she wanted at that moment. My wife had developed a lot of courage from what I had seen.

She will be a worthy wife and mother of our demons. She doesn't see it that way now. But the moment Moriah holds our first one in her arms, she won't see anyone but that little demon in front of her. I have wanted to live that moment since I saw her. See how my firstborn will be born from her womb. I will hold it in my hands and offer it to the darkness.

Then I will do the same with the next and the next until my wife can't take it anymore. And to have this future, I need to take care of her, as if she were the most delicate and precious object. I will face anyone who tries to steal my future from me. But for now, that's where and how I wanted to be. Breathing in her essence, feeling her energy through my skin, blending us. With this in mind, I closed my eyes and let the darkness embrace me.

****

My eyes suddenly opened, and I let out a moan at the same time. That's when I figured out what was going on. My head swelled with blood. Moriah held my member between her lips. The vision that I saw of her, with blood dripping from her mouth. It was the most erotic experience I have ever seen. I sat up at the speed of lightning and took her in my arms. I sucked on her lips, tasting her delicious blood, then licked the drops that had dripped down her neck.

Moriah, moaned every time my tongue touched her skin. She needed more from me, and I was going to give it to her. I gently pushed her to lie down. As she stared at me, she had those hungry eyes that provoked me so much. Afterwards, I brought my arm to my mouth and stuck my fangs into my skin. My forearm was soaked in blood. And spilt onto my chest and then trickled down to my abdomen. Then a small puddle formed at the base of my member. Moriah raised her head in astonishment, but her eyes said it all. She was starving, so I grabbed her from behind her head and held her close to my chest.

It didn't take long for her to start licking and sucking everything. At the touch of her tongue, my skin tickled, but she went even further and started sucking on my nipples. And with her small, human teeth, she bit me, and hard. Suddenly, I wished she would bite off all my skin. But I had to control myself. She is still a human, and until she receives the tattoo, I would have to wait. Following the bloodline with her tongue, she stopped when there was not a drop left.

Upon reaching my member. I screamed viscerally as she licked and sucked harder. After I couldn't take it anymore, I grabbed her hair and lifted her face. It was at that moment when I saw her that I knew she was mine, and I was hers.

Her face was covered in blood, and her tongue was cleaning her lips. Savouring it, tasting it. The wild, primal expression on her face was a testament to her instinct. I, still holding her head by the hair, brought my mouth closer to hers. And without waiting for a second more, I devoured it. That day, I made her scream like she never had before. Our bodies found the pleasure that many seeks, but very few find it. I can say that I took her to heaven many times, but I made sure she returned to hell with me.

Fill her belly with my seeds. Which were so many, that every time she moved I could see and hear how my vitality came out of her. My wife enjoyed every second of our encounter. My blood turned her into a true animal without a conscience. Just like me.

But it is time for Moriah to morph into something else. I don't want to keep wasting my time anymore. Her uterus is infertile until the tattoo comes to life. This dream, I don't want to put it off any longer. After thinking all this, I turned to see Moriah. She was with her head on my chest, caressing me. This is how I always want to see her, devoted to me, that I am the only thing that revolves around her. Although that will not be entirely possible. My babies will need their mother, and I will never deny them that.

I grab her chin with my fingers and bring her face to mine. Moriah looked at me closely, as if she was reading my mind. Then, she said, "What is in your mind? You are thinking very hard, and I have the suspicion that what you are thinking involves me." And with a cheeky smile, she continued, "So please tell me, before I put you inside me again and make you come all day." I couldn't help but laugh at her occurrences. In disbelief, she shook her head from side to side. However, she waits for me to say what I was thinking. "Moriah, as well as every other member of the royal family. You need to perform the ritual. A specific tattoo will be drawn on your skin. And for each member, it is different. We will then witness its manifestation when the darkness possesses you. Only in that way, you can receive the Persephone crown."

As Moriah gazed at me in hesitation, I continued. "I won't say that you will not suffer, but you have already endured a lot of pain. Therefore, you have nothing to fear." The gravity of the situation made my eyes harden. "If the darkness doesn't think you are good enough for me, the tattoo will not come to life, and you will die."

She sat up and turned her face to the other side. I was already feeling her absence with this simple fact. So I grabbed her by the arm and pushed her towards my body again. We were inches away from touching. Then she spoke, "You should have told me this before, what to do now Armaloth? If I fail, I will die, and then what?"

I looked into her eyes, and I knew she was disappointed. So I grabbed her face with both my hands and kissed her. When we finished the kiss, I put her head on my chest and stroked her hair. "You have nothing to worry about, my wife. There is nothing so far that you have not been able to achieve. Your strength is what my ancestors sought, and you, my wife, have it all." She looked off into nothingness, surely processing my words. Then she turned her gaze to mine and nodded her head, letting me know that she understood what she had to do. I smirked, at this. She is so tenacious, then said, "It's time. Time for the new queen to rise."

****

I could feel Moriah's concern. But I had not the slightest doubt that she would make it. It is one of her qualities. No matter what, she will get to the end. She is not one of those who give up when things get tough. The words

I said to Moriah were still reverberating in her mind. As she was silent, I decided to calm her mind. As I sat up from the floor, I looked at Moriah and said, "Come with me, wife, I know something will help you feel at ease." I stretched my hand, offering it to her, and without hesitation, Moriah took it and helped her up. She shows me a lot of her trust, which I find very encouraging. She followed me to the pond, and I went in first.

My arms spread out in her direction, and she fell into them. I took her in my arms easily and carried her to the centre of the pond. I submerged our bodies until only our heads were left out. Furthermore, I began to wash her body with my hand, leaving no space uncleared. Then I put water on her head and started with her hair. I never imagined enjoying this simple act so much. Moriah was taking everything from me. And I could only watch from a distance without doing anything. Perhaps this is the power of the chosen one. The true Persephone.

After finishing with her whole body, we were enjoying the water. Until she told me, "You know? This place brings back very bad memories. If I could be elsewhere, I would be." She said it without lifting her head, she had it resting on my shoulder. Contemplate what she said for a few seconds. And then, I remembered what she told me about making me happy.

This is nothing, and if this little detail keeps her with me, I will. So I replied, "This is the safest place in the entire underworld. Only I can have the power to enter or allow someone to enter. But after today. As a result, you will no longer be vulnerable to anyone. In fact, your power and strength will be greater than those of the general demons."

I took her chin in my fingers and lifted her face. Her eyes shone with many emotions, but I managed to make out one, Strength. My queen has a will of steel, and the tenacity of a warrior. I brought my mouth to hers and took her sweet lips with my fangs. I bit her lightly and then kissed her. Never in my existence had I experienced this, I don't even know what to call it. But I never want to lose this.

"So, my wife, after today and if you behave well, you will be able to choose where our new chamber will be." Ah! There it is, that mischievous smile. Moriah laughed lightly and said to me, "That, I will, my king, if I get out of this alive. You will have a long list to please. " I kissed her head and said, "It's time." I took her by the hand, and we walked out of the pond.

After summoning my slave, Anton. He immediately materialized and kneeled down, touching the floor with his forehead. " My master and my lady, your servant is here to serve you." And I informed him of everything that had to be done. After I turned to see my wife, I knew I had nothing to worry about, but I couldn't help it. So I hugged her and said, "Go with Anton, wife, do everything he tells you. We have to leave here, but I'll see you when the ritual is over."

She nodded her head and followed Anton. I, for my part, transported myself to the throne chamber. My thorny branches received me as always, wrapping themselves around me. My faithful Agalariept was there too. I could feel through the bond, that they were confident, they knew what was going to happen. But they had no doubt that my wife would make it. The three of us stayed in the throne chamber, mixing and sharing our energy. The rest of the time that remained before the ceremony, we spent observing our empire. I could see that our enemies were neutralized, and the heavens had no interference in my affairs.

It is at this very moment that I felt two powerful presences materialize before me. The mighty soul-eater dragon was the first to appear. His immense figure was occupying most of the space. Seeing me, he exhaled fumes from his nose and bowed his head in reverence. But only for a few seconds, as this creature does not respect his king.

With regard to the second presence, there had been no contact with her many centuries before. She materialized, and seeing her again reminded me how beautiful and powerful she is. Thankfully, she lives with the gods, so although she is my mother, she has not been eaten by the darkness. "Hecate, you honour me with your presence."

She approached me, smiled, and bowed her head in respect to the king of the underworld when she saw me. I stood from my throne and walked over to where she was standing. I offered her my hand, and she took it without hesitation. "Mother, I haven't seen you for a long time." Then she replied with a smile, "King of the underworld, my son, I apologize for not being able to come more often. But now I have an excuse to escape Olympus," she continued.

"You know that overprotective uncle of yours does not take his eyes off me." Yes, my uncle, Zeus, took his role as a protector very seriously. I was about to say something else when my servant materialized in front of me. Then he informed me that everything was ready. My insides twisted upon hearing this.

The time had come for my wife Moriah to lose her humanity. And giving way to immortality.

Chapter 15

Persephone
Moriah

This demon is called Anton, I remember him. In order not to scare me, he disguised himself as a human. "Anton," I called him by name, and he made a priceless face when he heard it. That makes me laugh so hard I can hardly stand up. The demon reached down and put his forehead on the floor, singing "My lady." I was waiting to see what he would do, but he remained in the same position.

"Get up Anton. Do you know? I remember you, and I know that face is not yours. " Anton, surprised, obeyed me and nervously told me "My lady, I don't want to scare you with my true form. I know how sensitive you are, and from experience, I have to tell you that you wouldn't like to see it."

Poor devil, I have to end his suffering. "I know, before, it was all new, but after seeing my husband and the dragon demon, I think you are child's play." The demon blushed, if that's possible. "My lady, as you wish," He shook his head and his true face appeared. Oh! OK, He warned me, and I didn't listen to him. But this would be my new life, and I would have to get used to these kinds of visions.

So in a nonchalant voice, I said, "You're not so bad," And I dare to fake a smile. Apparently, I made his day with this comment, because he gave me a huge smile, and it really was huge. His mouth almost reached from one ear to the other. Phew! I removed this image from my head, and better, I decided to bring up the subject of the ceremony or rite. Or whatever they call it.

"Now tell me, Anton, what do you want me to do?" The demon put his hands together and said, "My lady, I want to tell you something very important." His seriousness in saying this put me on guard, but I let him continue. "I know you are not used to many things, but what you will go through in a few moments may shock you. For what I advised you, keep calm."

OK, I knew it would be difficult, but now I don't know what to expect. The ancestors of the almighty king dwell in the well of doom. Their spirits must decide what tattoo you will receive, so you must stay there. You will be marked by their energy and by the design they have chosen for you. You can leave when the tattoo has been completed on your skin."

"But that is only the beginning. The tattoo must come to life if you want to be crowned by my Lord. And that's the second part of the ritual. The ritual will take place in the ritual chamber. You've already been there when you were baptized by the blood of the innocents. "Oh, no, not there." My face must have said it all because Anton just moved his head up and down.

"While there, My Lord will call the power of darkness to activate the tattoo. But you, my lady, you will have to be very brave and strong. Since darkness usually consumes even the strongest. The darkness seeks your vulnerability and exploits it. Making you fall into despair. Those who do not succeed will end up destroyed, and their souls will wander eternally in nothingness." The only thing I understand perfectly is that my life could end in a few more hours, and in the worst way. I looked down at the floor, contemplating my options. Armaloth is very sure that I will pass this rite, and that the tattoo will come to life. But I'm not so sure.

Anton tells me to follow him. We go through several tunnels, until we reach a door with some rather terrifying inscriptions. I didn't know what it was, but I felt it in my bones. That it was something that would give me nightmares for a long time if I managed to survive at all. When Anton inserted the key into the lock, the door opened, and I waited for him to enter with me, but he only watched me and with his head, he refused. From this point forward, I was by myself. As I looked ahead, I was unable to breathe due to absolute darkness. It was impossible for me to breathe. I was also paralysed from the waist down, and even if I tried to move, I could not.

But Anton whispered encouraging words in my ear that made me react. I swallowed hard, and took my first step forward, then the other, and then another. The place was instantly lit up with torches, pointing me the way I had to go. The path led me to spiral staircases that led downward. I took my time walking down the steps, and the lower I got, the more air was scarce. And the place just got colder. After descending many steps, I finally stepped onto the ground. And as its name indicated, it was the bottom of a well. This was the place.

There was nothing around me, just the stone walls and steps leading up to the surface. Other than that, nothing else. At that moment, I began to feel as if the ground caught my feet. It was pulling me in, and I could not escape. I was screaming hysterically at that point. The only thing on my mind is that I was going to die, buried alive. But something managed to pass that fog of despair. *"My daughter is very intelligent and always knows how to overcome any obstacle."* It's the only thing in my thoughts.

My brain went blank, and I only listened to the sweet words that my father said to me. *My daughter is very intelligent and always knows how to overcome any obstacle."* My mind immediately calmed down, and only then was I able to relax my body. Whatever happens, my mind will go in peace. So let my body be dragged to the ground. My whole body was buried in an instant.

There was no oxygen for me to breathe. I only had a few seconds for my body to start demanding air. And with my eyes closed, I thought about everything I did in my life. How satisfied I was with everything I accomplished. For all the love that my father gave me and I gave him. I thanked him a thousand times for being my father and vowed that I would see him again. I also thought of Armaloth. The last days with him were as I had never imagined. Not only that, but I also thought about how much I would like to continue cultivating our relationship. And someday, it would become love so strong that it would transcend the worlds.

I also thought of my fire horse and my thorny branches. How much they would miss me if I didn't come back. While I was thinking about all this. My body has been grasped by many hands. And I ran out of oxygen. Then, my body began to float.

After that, I don't know what happened, because when I opened my eyes, I was lying at the bottom of the well. As if nothing had happened. And then, I saw a light in the distance, which blinded me. I got up off the ground and tried to cover the glare from my eyes. But I decided, better, to follow the light. I walked around for a while until I saw where it came from.

I approached cautiously, and at that moment, I remembered where I was. It was the chamber of sacrifices. The place I feared the most. So I walked to the circle that was in the middle of everything and looked around me. But I wasn't expecting what I saw in front of me.

Armaloth was sitting on his thorny throne. Watching me very carefully. I could feel even his emotions. He was as agitated as I was. On the other side, was the dragon, fuming from its nose. With the same boring face as ever. That made me smile slightly. And next to him, there was a very beautiful woman. I could see that she was not human, nor a demon.

But I did feel her power. And it was huge, my skin crawled just looking at her. I also saw demons that I had never seen, and they were massive. This place was the concentration of evil. And I was in the middle of everyone. While I was looking around me. The circles on the floor, lit up one by one, up to the circle where I was. Afterwards, everything was silent. I turned to see my husband, but he was not moving. Suddenly, the audience turned to look at him, expectant. Until I saw Armaloth stand up. His intense gaze was on me, and I couldn't take my eyes off him. But after a time. He closed his eyes and raised his arms. I could clearly see how two black spheres were forming in each hand.

And he shot them at me. I was with eyes wide open in surprise until I felt a blow, and then the other. The black balls penetrated my skin. And that's when I felt my body freeze. That energy was taking over my body. I could feel myself losing against that energy. Something terrible was happening to me, my life was slipping away from me. I was being sucked up by this darkness. I was losing my memory, I was raving. Not only that, but I had no idea what I was doing. Who am I?

"ARRR!" I heard a roar in the distance, but that sound was coming from me. I felt like my body was changing, transforming into something sinister, dangerous and deadly. CRACK! Furthermore, I heard my bones thundering. "AAAHHH!" I arch my back from the pain. It was excruciating, my legs gave out, and I fell to my knees. Then it was my neck, something was squeezing me, with titanic force. The pressure caused my nerves to explode and my spine to shatter. My head hung from my neck without strength. And my arms dangled by my sides, my whole body fell to the floor like a rag.

My mind was in pain, all the nerve endings were bleeding. My organs had exploded too. It was a deformed mass of flesh, as there was not a single bone that could hold its shape. But my suffering had not stopped, the black balls of energy came out of me. And to finish me off, they started beating my body from the outside. By now, I could tell I was dead. My conscience was the last thing left. And it could disappear at any time. Until I couldn't see anything, I couldn't hear anything, and I no longer felt the pain. The only thing I could perceive was a buzzing. ZZZZZZ! ZZZZZZ! And then darkness ....

I opened my eyes and blinked several times. I noticed that I was floating as if my body did not weigh, and nothing was dragging me down. Everything was at peace here. I didn't have to worry about anything. So I let my body go freely through space. After all, I could say that I finally reached peace.

I was floating in nothingness for a long time until I saw a glow approaching. I was very intrigued. What could it be? Raise my head to see better and make out a silhouette. As it got closer, I could see that he was a man, and very old. He had half his hair and his skin was wrinkled. But his body was a bit curved. But he didn't seem to suffer from anything.

He kept moving until he was standing in front of me just a few feet away. And he smiled at me, it was so warm, and I heard a sound inside me *"bat......dum"*, I didn't know what it was, but I felt it. He shook his head slightly and said, "Moriah, now are you the one who doesn't remember me?" The old man told me.

I didn't understand anything, of course, I don't know who he is. I shook my head as a sign that I did not know, him, so he puffed something frustrated. "Moriah, I need you to remember what I told you the day, that you discovered that you weren't ageing." I stared at him puzzled. I even moved my head a little to the side. The old man shook his head, "May I touch your hand?" The old man asked me and

I nodded my head, he closed the distance that separated us and grabbed my hand.

And I felt it again, that sound *"ba-dum"* One after another, images from my past life returned to my mind. *"Ba-dum, ba-dum".* Until I found the one I was looking for. *"My daughter is very intelligent and always knows how to overcome any obstacle." "This you just did is brilliant, worthy of my daughter, we will do it your way." "Everything will be fine, you can do it"*

That old man was my father, the person I most needed in the world, the only one who took care of my back until the end, The reason for my existence. And he had abandoned me, for the first time in my life. He abandoned me, but neither he nor I could do anything. "Dad, you left me alone, do you know how much it hurt to see you go? How much do I miss you?"

"Take me with you, look," And with my arms open, I pointed around me. "Here, I am alone" But my dad smiled at me, and said, "Yes, daughter, here you are very alone." He said that looking around. "But you can't come with me. That place was not meant for you, even though you were the best, and you helped so many people. But your destiny is elsewhere. And there is also someone who is waiting for you. He trusts that you will return to him, that you will find your way back home." Home, where is my home.

"Ba-dum, ba-dum, ba-dum" "Think Moriah Regina, why are you here?" My dad looked me in the eye waiting for an answer, and it was on the tip of my tongue. But everything was very complicated and blurry. Still, I managed to

remember a voice telling me, "*my queen, Moriah of Armaloth, my wife*"

"*Ba-dum, ba-dum, ba-dum, ba-dum*" "Armaloth," I yelled suddenly. My dad nodded his head, smiling at the same time. And his body began to slowly move away. I looked him in the eye, begging him not to leave me. My tears were shed without me knowing how it happened. "*Everything will be fine, you can do it.*" I managed to hear his words for the last time. Just as I smiled at him for the last time, too.

Afterwards, the light he brought left with him as well. Leaving me in the dark again. But he had left something. The knowledge of what I was and what I wanted to do. So I wasted no more time. And I began to imagine myself in Armaloth's arms, his face, his presence. His kisses. And I began to invoke his name over and over again, and in the middle of that darkness, an immense force was nesting in the midst of my chest.

The power was unstoppable, and a ray of light shot from my centre, like an arrow, pointing the way. I followed it despite the darkness surrounding me. Never once did I take my eyes off that light. I was getting closer now, I could sense it. My husband was waiting for me at home. There it is, as the light grows until the darkness disappears.

When I opened my eyes, I found myself lying on the ground. The glassy eyes of Armaloth were staring at me. When he saw I opened mine, his face froze for a few moments, then he bent down hiding his head in my hair and said in a low voice, "You are alive, you are alive." His anguish was undeniable. When I looked around, I saw onlookers standing silently, wide-eyed. To not keep them waiting any longer, I whispered into Armaloth's ear to help me get up. Although my body had been beaten, I didn't feel pain. In fact, the strength I felt inside was growing by the second.

As soon as I got up, I straighten my back and lift my head. My husband's gaze was filled with pride as he contemplated me. I couldn't believe what had happened. Despite all that, here I was. "Death was no match for me," I whispered to myself. But at that moment, my back began to heat up, and the power that I had felt in me was overflowing. I squeezed Armaloth's hand, and he nodded his head, hinting to let him go. And when I did, the power in my body exploded, and from my back, I could feel my skin tear apart.

Then, I saw the most beautiful thorny branches I had ever seen coming out from me. They began to snake around me, entangling themselves in my husband's legs, arms, head. Then I remember the tattoo that my husband's ancestors chose for me, but now I knew what it was. The tattoo had finally come to life.

This display of affection from my thorny branches made Armaloth smile. And from his chest, a silver crown emerged. As soon as I saw it, I knew it was the queen's crown. I lowered my head and in that way, my husband Armaloth, king of the underworld, crowned me as queen Persephone. The one who would reign alongside him for eternity.

The end

Epilogue

The training
Moriah

"**N**o Moriah, you're doing it all wrong. That's not how I told you to do it." Oh! Please. This is the fifth or sixth time I've tried it, and nothing seems to satisfy this grumpy old dragon. "We will do it again, and this time I want you to focus like never before. You need to free those thorny branches and stop them at the moment I tell you to. Did you hear me, Moria? This time you have to stop them. I have no more humans left to practice with." I lowered my gaze and saw the five practice targets on the ground. What insignificant and pathetic beings.

And only thinking that I was one of them once. I don't know how Armaloth could have noticed me. The god of the underworld and a human? Ridiculous. But in the end, that's how things turned out. And here I am, after more than a year of being crowned queen of the underworld. And despite the time, I haven't been able to fully master my powers. It seems that my human part continues to interfere with some things.

Dragon has told me that my human emotions have not been completely eradicated. And that he doesn't know if I'll get rid of them completely. I have no idea what's so bad about still having those traces of humanity. Now that I'm a demon, I don't need anything to interfere with my new world. The time I have lived here has taught me that dominion and power are the things that will save me from others. My husband is with me and I will always have his support. But he also let me know that I have to defend myself and give myself respect.

A queen must be able to command all her servants with power and authority. That's what they told me. And in a certain way, it is true. The demons think they can get favours from me by trying to manipulate me. The level we are talking about is higher than I could have believed. As a human, I have never been exposed to such evil. Not even the tricks that are so easily used here.

And if my humanity is holding me back from reaching my potential, I will do everything I can to rid myself of it. Not only for me, but for my family. I need to be at my best to be able to protect them. Hell is not a place where you can afford to rest for a few days. No, I have learned from the various attacks on my person that I can never let my guard down. Fortunately, Armaloth has been there to prevent any harm. "Once more Moriah." The dragon's voice snapped me out of my thoughts. "You will not be able to get out of here until you manage to contain your thorny branches. You need to control them especially when you are with Armaloth. That display of affection they have for him is embarrassing." Ugh! The dragon is right. I am ashamed of myself. My thorny branches do not miss an opportunity to get entangled on him at any time. And I haven't been able to command them when Armaloth is near me. They just don't obey.

"Ready?" I nodded my head. And place my attention on the human target in front of me. "NOW." Hearing the signal, I let my thorny branches come out from behind my back. I concentrated on the attack, and the intensity and speed. "STOP" I closed my fists and clenched them tightly. Grinding my teeth, I forced the force pouring out of me to stop. The site was silent.

I had closed my eyes to concentrate better, and when I opened them again, I saw what had happened. I turned to see the dragon, and it was fuming from his nostrils. His face held a ridiculous smirk. But for me, I wasn't behind. I turned to see my target again, and he was white with shock. Sweat ran down his entire face. And his chest rose and fell painfully. But that wasn't what caught my attention. It was my thorny branches that were inches away from piercing his neck. I was so close to failure. But HEY! I made it.

"Ha, ha, ha. The dragon is laughing. His laugh seemed more like he was choking. And not only that, his nostrils exhaled smoke with every laugh he gave. A few seconds later, the place looked like the streets of London in 1820. You couldn't see beyond your nose. I fanned the smoke with my hand to get it away from my face. But it was impossible to get rid of this one. "Stop dragon, you're going to kill us all." Finally, the laughter stopped. And the dragon squeezed his eyelids freeing himself of the tears that blinded him.

The smoke disappeared little by little, letting us see again. I turned to see the dragon, and it had a cynic grin. As if this was the funniest thing that had ever happened to him. I shook my head annoyed. Idiot dragon. Taking a step forward, I bumped into something. I looked down and saw that it was the human I hadn't killed.

I turned to see what the dragon was saying. "Here is your last human, and you did this all by yourself. He suffocated to death." Dragon blew smoke out of his nose saying. "There is nothing more to do. Your husband will have to replenish my slaves. In this dimension, it's not easy to get them, you know?" I shrugged nonchalantly, it was his problem. "My child, do not let this dragon bother you. You have to understand that he is very old and would do anything to play a joke on you." Hecate said looking the dragon straight in the eye. He wrinkled his nose and fumed, but said nothing.

"It's not exactly the dragon Hecate. The truth is that I don't want to get home yet. I want to keep practising. But it's really hard to master my powers. I need to become powerful. I'm already tired of the attacks against me. No one respects me, and it's about time to change that." Hecate looked at me moving her head slightly to the side. She got up from the rock she was sitting on and walked towards me. When she reached me, she took me by the shoulders, saying. "Moriah, you are a little over a year old. In the demon world, age weighs heavily. Power increases over the years. I'm sorry to tell you that you won't achieve much. Your powers will grow to the measure, and you will be able to handle them as you please, but that will take time. You need to be patient and remember that my son will always be there for you. Do not despair."

I nodded my head and put one of my hands in hers. She smiled and turned back to the same rock she was sitting on. "Now let's start again," Hecate said clapping her hands. And a dozen humans appeared out of nowhere. OKAY. This day is going to be long.

They have to learn

Armaloth

"No, Prince Badaloth. No, your father the king will ask for my head." With great pride, I watch from my throne as my son Badaloth gives Anton a terrible day. My little boy is proving to be a full-fledged devil. He is barely a year and a half old and his powers are magnificent. My relics did well to choose their mother. Moriah, my wife. Remembering her name made me wonder what she was doing? She has been in the dragon dimension for over a week. And it's about time she returned to fulfil her obligations. I raise my hand closing my eyes.

I started to generate a black cloud in front of me. A portal appeared in front of me, and I commanded my thorny branches through the portal. They crossed dimensions until they reached their goal. When I had it, I ordered them back. "AAAAA!" From the portal, Moriah's screams were heard while she was dragged from the dragon dimension into my presence. I could hear her nearer. Seconds later, my wife's body was dragged over to me. My thorny branches gently deposited her on the ground.

She raised her face and she looked angry. My queen was not happy. "Armaloth, I've already told you not to do that. You embarrass me in front of others. How is it possible that this idea crosses your mind? Treating the queen like this is not right. Now I begin to see why no one respects me." I threw my head back laughing out loud. With a wave of my hand, my thorny branches dragged her towards me. Her body bumped into mine. When I had her in front of me, I took her by the waist and pulled her closer to my body. Moriah let out an involuntary groan. Her face was in front of mine. And her eyes were on mine. "My queen, who am I?" I asked her quietly. Moriah was looking at me intently. And little by little, I began to feel her thorny branches zigzagging and snaking at my feet. Then slowly climb up my leg.

Her energy began to circulate in me. I felt her desire, her anger, and her love. And yes, she loves me. It is part of her nature as a human. That is the only thing that will remain of her humanity. Her love for me. Moria closed her eyes and opened them instantly. She took a breath and said. "You are the king of the underworld Armaloth. My king and husband." She stood on tiptoe and kissed me softly on the mouth.

I immediately took control of the kiss devouring her. A week without my wife by my side, that can't be any more. One week. That dragon is taking a lot of liberties. I ended the kiss and was about to tell her that I didn't want her to spend any more time with the dragon. But out of the corner of my eye, I saw how my son Madaloth came towards us at full speed.

I was sure he wanted to catch his mother off guard like so many other times by falling on top of her. I was about to hold him back when Moriah surprised me by raising her arm in our son's direction. Madaloth was suspended in the air without being able to move. The little devil moved furiously trying to escape from the force field that was containing him. Moriah winked at me and I turned to look at him. She moved her hand and tossed the little annoyance to the other wall of the throne room. Madaloth bounced like a ball from one side to the other. Until after a while it stopped. My son was stunned in the bubble that it continued to contain him.

But that was not all. Badaloth who was busy destroying the door realized that his mother had arrived. He hurriedly jumped towards her. Remiloth and Mordoloth came out from behind the throne of thorns with a great leap as well. My little ones can feel the presence of their mother immediately. But none of them had the opportunity to jump on top of their mother as usual. Moriah without even looking shot her energy at each of them, enveloping them in bubbles.

My children fought with claws and teeth to free themselves, but all was in vain. Moriah did to all of them what she did to Madaloth. She tosses them to the other side of the wall, so they bounce across the entire length of the throne room. I kept my eyes wide open. How did she learn these tricks? How did the dragon teach her to do that?

Observe my children giddy inside the spheres. But the surprising thing is that after the shake, they stayed put. I smiled at my wife showing my fangs. I grabbed her hand and led her towards her throne. When she took her seat, I did the same in mine. Our thorny branches snaked all over the place, tangling with each other. When Moria saw that our demons had enough, she popped the bubbles. One by one, they got up from the ground and in a peaceful way, walked towards where their mother was. I couldn't believe it, even Anton was stunned in one of the corners of the room.

My wife's thorny branches snake around our children lifting them up. They were carrying them into Moriah's lap. Once seated there, they all looked up at their mother. They were waiting for orders. My jaw dropped. My demons since they were born all together have been a real threat. None of them could miss the opportunity to harass their mother or jump on her, one by one or all together.

They were able to make the most trained demons runaway from my palace. They are a real pest. But this? I guided my gaze towards Moriah trying to understand what was going on. My wife saw our demons and nodded her head. They wasted no time and climbed onto her. Moriah hugged and kissed them one by one. Her thorny branches zigzagged excitedly around them. Moriah couldn't help it. Any expression of love and affection towards us, and this was the result.

My children after a while remained calm on their mother's lap. Moriah finally turned around with a smile on her face. "What did you do?" That was the only thing I could ask her. She made a satisfying pout with her mouth and said. "The bubbles were a little trick I learned from your mother." Hecate was with the dragon? My face must have said it all. She only nodded her head and continued. "That's right, beloved husband. Your mother gave me very good advice on how to deal with badly behaved imps." She winked at me again. "She told me so many stories about how she practically had to leave you and your brothers in the bubbles for hours. Until all of you finally calmed down."

I shook my head in annoyance. How dare my mother reveal such embarrassing things about my childhood? But Moriah continued. "The rest, I figured it out by myself." That piqued my interest. "What do you mean you figured it out on your own?"

"Yes, husband. Remember the prophecy?"

"What?" I replied in disbelief.

Moriah smiled saying. "The prophecy says that a human and the king of the underworld will give life to the invincible army. But nowhere does it say who commanded that army. Everyone assumes that it will be the king. But now, I discovered something very important today when I was training with the dragon. My humanity will not be completely lost. For that, I would have to stop loving. And by loving I won't be able to have as much power as you, demons. But there is something on my side to make up for that loss."

Moriah was surprising me more and more with what she was saying. "What is it? Tell me." I couldn't help but ask.

"My children. The invincible army can only be commanded by the mother. My sons and daughters will obey only me. They won't let anything bad happen to me. They will take care of me and protect me with all their demonic power. Even from you, my love."

I grabbed Moriah by the back of her neck and pulled her face close to mine. And with my penetrating sight, I asked her. "And who commands you?"

Moriah swallows hard and blinks several times. But after a few seconds, a gorgeous smile spread all over her face. "You, my husband and king. You command me."

Satisfied with her response, I attacked her mouth with mine. If a few years ago someone had told me that my being would belong to a human. Certainly, I would have destroyed them in seconds by the insult. Moriah, my wife, and my children are the most important thing in my kingdom. They are everything. We will fulfil the prophecy together. We will conquer the worlds and become known as the kingdom that conquered all. The underworld. When they hear our names, even Olympus and heavens will tremble.

Social media

Visit my blog
https://www.vioshedbooks.com

Visit my Pinterest
www.pinterest.com/vioshedbooks

Visit my Amazon store

E-mail me
vioshed@outlook.com

Books In This Series

Empire of Thorns

Moriah was one of the most prestigious psychiatrists in the country, until the king of the underworld, stepped his eyes on her. Her life stopped being perfect, having visions and hearing voices.

After successfully treating what she believed to be mental illness, the real challenge came when Armaloth himself took her in broad daylight.

Pain and suffering is the only thing that awaits you in the kingdom of the god of the underworld. Envy and jealousy surround the king's court, along with legendary creatures with ancient powers.

Moriah has to survive in her new life and accept that the King will never let her go. She believes that her suffering will have no end. Life in the Underworld is slowly killing her. All her hopes and will to leave are fading away. Nothing matters but to fulfil her destiny.

The fight between heaven and hell can break out at any moment. Armaloth will do whatever it takes to make the prophecy come true, and not even the god above himself will stand in his way.

The Thorns King's Wife: The Trapped Bride

The Thorn's Mark: The Willing Queen

Books By This Author

Wasn't My Love Enough?: What Would You Do For Love?

Sail along with Sandra, Terry and Frank through this passionate and painful story. Where loyalties are measured, Some wills are imposed, and the love promises of youth are put to the test.

Wasn't My Love Enough?: I Would Do Everything For Love

andra cannot accept what is happening to her. They are destroying the world that she has created with pain and tears. Terry and Frank have lost their minds. They have taken over her entire life. But both of them are determined to follow their strategy to the letter to recover Sandra's love. No matter how painful it is.

Nora And Erik: When We Were Nothing

Nora was part of a transaction her father and Erik agreed upon. Already married for five years, Nora is lonely and desperate. The life, she thought, is nowhere near reality. The life of crime, and the unbridled carnal excesses that her husband lives, are dangerously bordering her on the brink of despair. Betrayed by her family, and by her husband. Nora wants to find a way out of this unwanted life, and one day finds love.

Nora And Erik: When Our Souls Intertwined

Nora thought that she had finally found her way to happiness. But her whole life fell apart in a matter of minutes. Alone and pregnant, Nora will have to face the person she fears the most from her past. Discover the future that awaits Nora. Where betrayals and misfortunes are just around the corner. And revenge is the main dish.